The Brand Inheritance

Dorothy Fletcher

CRIMSON
ROMANCE
F+W Media, Inc.

This edition published by
Crimson Romance
an imprint of F+W Media, Inc.
10151 Carver Road, Suite 200
Blue Ash, Ohio 45242
www.crimsonromance.com

CHAPTER ONE

The plane landed at Kennedy Airport at eight o'clock in the evening, daylight saving time. The stream of passengers, disgorged from the belly of the ship, trudged across the sun-lit field, tired but starry-eyed, and straggled into the TWA arrivals center. There was a scramble for luggage carts, a bedlam of voices. Up above, waving through glass windows, were people waiting to welcome vacationing friends and relatives. *But not for me*, Margo thought as she lined up at Customs.

"Anything to declare?"

Bags zipped open, the line moving slowly, inexorably. "Is this a new coat?" No air conditioning, and for a June evening it was warm and humid. "Does it have to take all *night?*" someone muttered, wiping his forehead with a wilted handkerchief. "Move ahead, please," a Customs official said crisply.

The tall girl with the wheat-colored hair made a move to lift one of her suitcases to the counter. "That's top heavy for you," the man behind her said. "Let me give you an assist."

"How kind of you," she said, perspiring.

"Not at all."

He hefted her three suitcases to the counter. "You don't travel light," he remarked, smiling.

"I've been living abroad. Thanks, I know they're like lead."

"Will you share my cab back to town?"

"Thanks very much," she said, surveying him. Fiftyish, a good, honest face, nothing to worry about. "I'd be delighted," she said gratefully.

"Good girl. I live in the East Fifties. I can drop you wherever."

"Perfect," she said.

"Whereabouts are you going?"

"I don't know, I don't live anywhere," she said, and saw his startled eyes. At the Inspector's request, she opened her first suitcase. The man, out of long experience, searched through it, scarcely disturbing the contents. He closed the grip, put a chalk mark on it, and started on the second, his fingers deft. In due time that too was zipped up. Then the third, which was books and letters and photography equipment. "Is this a new camera?" the Customs Inspector asked.

"No, it's not new at all; as I said, I've nothing to declare."

"How long was your visit?"

"Thirteen years."

His head shot up. "You're an American citizen?"

"Yes I am."

He gave her a quick, appraising look, then smiled pleasantly and said, "Welcome back, Miss."

"Thanks very much," she said, and the man behind her spoke imperatively. "Just wait outside the gate," he said. "I won't be long."

"It's very good of you."

"No bother at all."

She stood there waiting, and shortly he joined her. "I'll just get a cab," he said, and was back in no time at all. "Here we go." The black porter slung the bags on a cart, eeled his way past the throngs. The cool, shadowy evening was very lovely, though somehow perplexing. She was accustomed to French, Italian, Spanish airports; there was a difference here, a hard, pitiless quality. But this was home! After many a wandering, like Ulysses, she had returned, and she looked out the wndow of the cab, saw clustering groups embracing and gesturing. "Where to?" the driver asked.

"Manhattan," the man said. "When we get there I'll tell you the address."

"Yes, sir."

He leaned back and took a pack of cigarettes from his pocket, shook one out for her. "Thanks," she said, and he lit it with a Dunhill lighter. "Where am I taking you?" he asked.

"Oh, I suppose the St. Regis or the Plaza. What do you think?"

"Either. Of course I have a soft spot in my heart for the Plaza, but it's up to you. I heard you tell the Customs man you'd been away for thirteen years. Where?"

"At school, in Switzerland. When I left there I went to Paris, studied there too. Now I've come back to where I started. A job. Some free-lance work. Whatever I can find. A place to live."

She saw his eyes travel over her clothing, her well-cared-for person, and lifted a hand. "I'm twenty-one," she said. "It's time for me to make my own way. Life doesn't owe anyone a living."

"I see," he said, and she liked the look she saw on his face, a look of respect. "I have good training," she explained. "Now it's time for me to put it to use. But enough about me. Was your trip business or pleasure?"

"Business," he said. "I'm in import-export, I travel frequently. Sometimes my family goes with me, this time they didn't. I have a daughter your age, and a son who's married. I'm, in fact, a grandfather. I'm not sure I like being one. I suppose none of us likes to get old."

"You're not old at all."

"Thanks for the compliment; I'll treasure it."

They approached the bridge. "Have you decided where to stay?" the man asked.

"The Plaza. You said you had a soft spot for it, so the Plaza, then. You see, I'm a bit bewildered. I didn't think I'd feel so... so lost. But I do." She turned away and looked out the window, at the drab industrial buildings of Queens. "There were all those people at the airport," she said. "Arms stretched out, and glad faces. Coming home and being met with tears and laughter and flowers. It made me—"

"I can understand," he said.

"You seem to understand," she said steadily. "And I'll never forget you, or how you came to my aid. I can't thank you enough."

"The pleasure's mine," he said, warmly. "My name's Nelson Crawford, and I'd like very much to know yours."

"I'm Margo Brand."

They headed west, and the city lights were winking now. Tall buildings, taller than Margo remembered, looming against the evening sky. Glass and steel, intimidating. Wonderingly, she said, "It looks so different. I didn't remember it like this."

"It is different," Mr. Crawford said gravely. "It's different every year, every month."

"I'll have to get used to it."

"*I'm* not used to it. It's grown beyond me. Left me behind, if you will." They came to Park Avenue and she peered out the window, looking south. "What's that?" she asked, pointing.

"The Pan Am Building. An eyesore? Only one of many. I'll retire one of these days, go to Mallorca or some such place. I'll be happy to shake the dust of this misbegotten city off my—" He apologized a moment later. "Excuse me," he said contritely. "Don't let me discourage you. It's your city now, you young people. I'm sorry to have sounded off. Well, my dear, here we are."

They came to the lovely square just off 59th Street, facing the well-lit and hospitable hotel. Mr. Crawford leaned forward. "We'll get out here," he said, and fished in his wallet for a bill. "There you are," he said, "don't bother about the change, keep it."

"Thank you, sir," the cab driver said.

A porter dashed out of the hotel, dragging the suitcases from the trunk of the cab. A party of people dressed for an evening abroad came down the steps, headed for the parked taxi. "Hey, there ..."

The lobby was pleasant and spacious. Mr. Crawford, at the desk, said the young lady wished a room with bath.

"For how long a stay?" the desk clerk asked.

"Indefinitely," Margo said.

He consulted a room schedule. "I could give you a single with bath on the fourteenth floor. Twenty-seven dollars a day."

"Nothing less expensive?" Mr. Crawford asked.

"It's all right," Margo said.

"You're sure?"

"Yes, it's fine." She got out her traveler's checks and paid a week's rent in advance.

"Call if you need help," Mr. Crawford said.

"Oh no, everything's fine. My parents are very well-to-do. I'm only twenty-one, they're still responsible for me. It's my pride, you understand. I'm eager to be on my own. Meanwhile I have to accept their largesse."

"Where are your parents?" Mr. Crawford asked.

"In the East, doing research," she said. "I haven't seen them for ten years."

"For ten years?" he repeated, looking hard at her.

"Except for a day here and a day there. They're a well-known team of writers. You see, Mr. Crawford, I was an accident. They never wanted to have a child. They didn't need a child. I was only an embarrassment to them. I accepted that long ago. I'm sure you're in a hurry to get home to your family, Mr. Crawford, but before you go may I buy you a drink? I'd rather give you emeralds, but I'm afraid all the jewelry stores are closed. I wouldn't take up much of your time, but it would give me pleasure to…to buy you a drink."

"No no, I'll buy you a drink," he said, touched to the quick. "It isn't often I'm in the company of such a pretty girl." And over her protests he marched her back to one of the small salons and ordered champagne cocktails. "Unless you'd rather have something else?" he asked her.

"No no…but I do want to be host, Mr. Crawford."

He smiled, patted her hand, and was so deft at drawing her out that she told him a great deal about herself. "My parents? They're achievers, they travel all over the globe. I'm sorry I said that about my being an accident, it sounded cheap and cruel. I don't blame them one bit, they're so busy, and so famous."

She looked up. "And very, very much in love with each other."

And with themselves, Mr. Crawford thought, unable to imagine casting off his own daughter like some second-hand bit of goods. He looked across at the lovely, fresh face of the girl opposite him and thought, *This child was given everything…and nothing.*

"Actually, I had a very happy childhood," she said, as if she sensed his unspoken criticisms. "I spent many, many summers with a wonderful woman, and I must call her, now I'm back."

"Who's that?" Mr. Crawford asked.

"My aunt. Godmother and aunt. Victoria Brand. If anyone cares about me, she does."

"Tell me about her," he prompted. "Where does she live?"

"In a small country town, upstate, very pretty, you know, the hinterlands. All sorts of things going on up there, hexes and feuds and inbreeding and, like Salem, once witches were burned at the stake. I like it, have always liked it, because it makes me think of the beginnings of this country, and it's changed so little. I spent my summers there when I was a kid, and my Aunt Vicky practically brought me up. Her house is very historic, a landmark in the region; people come from all over to see it. It was wonderful for me as a child, I felt a part of history."

"I'm sure your aunt can't wait to hear from you."

"She doesn't expect me back until autumn. She'll be *very* astonished. I hope she won't have a heart attack when she hears my voice."

"Why a heart attack?"

"She's not young any more. Well, actually, she's my great-aunt. She's in her…I guess eighties by now."

"Rather than a heart attack, she'll undoubtedly start polishing the family silver," Mr. Crawford said with a broad smile. "That's what these landowners do for the returned prodigal, isn't it? And dust cobwebs off vintage wines …"

He was rewarded with a tinkling laugh. "I suppose," she said, chuckling. "She'll order everyone about and stalk through the house seeing that the antimicassars are in place, the old dear. I wish I had everything settled, so I could dash right up and be cosseted. But I must see to living quarters, and about a job…oh, no thanks, not another drink, this was lovely. And won't you let me treat? I have no other way to thank you for your kindness…for …"

She broke off. There was the sheen of tears behind the bewitching eyes. Then after a short silence she said composedly, "For welcoming me home. As if I had conjured you up out of a bottle, a genie, a hand in mine, just when I needed it."

He was very much moved. Passing this beautiful girl on the street anyone would think, *Lucky creature, with everything going for her …*

"You'll be all right?" he asked, back in the lobby again.

"Just fine. You took the sting out of…well, out of—"

In a kind of insane moment, like some Latin gigolo, he picked up her hand and kissed it. Feeling a little foolish, a little dotty. And then he went out and hailed a taxi, rather set-up and jaunty. It was a small adventure.

A man my age doesn't have many small adventures, he told himself, directing the driver to his Upper East Side address.

And oh, she had such fathomless eyes …

I should have given her my telephone number, he thought, starting to worry. *All alone, a stranger in this complex city …*

Yet an inner voice told him that the tall girl with the wheat-colored hair would make it on her own. That there was a kind of steely strength underneath that soft, feminine exterior. And, peeling off some bills to pay the cab driver, he climbed out and let himself into the lighted brownstone.

"Margaret?" he called. "Margaret. I'm home. I'm home, dear."

• • •

Her room was pleasant, lamp-lit, the bed turned down. She opened her overnight case, took out the necessary items, smoked a cigarette and then prepared for the night. A bath, her teeth brushed, and into a gauzy nightgown. She turned off the light, but the room was not really dark, the lights of Manhattan winking, blinking. She turned over, away from the window, facing the wall.

It was an old hotel, solidly built, but still there were sounds in the corridor, a buzz of voices, doors opening and closing. I'm too tired to sleep, she thought, but then she slept, and it was the gold of the new day that woke her. Disoriented, she had a moment of panic. Where was she?

And then she remembered. She was in New York City, at the Hotel Plaza, on her own, and in a city she had last seen thirteen years ago. *How will it treat me?* she wondered, and then she fell asleep again, simply to prolong the moment when she would have to get up and face the world, this new world from long ago, the forgotten city where she had been born; the strange, lost place where she had opened her eyes once upon a time. Babylon revisited.

• • •

At ten she called Cranford. She waited, fidgeting with the desk blotter, listening to the ringing. Her heart beat faster as she heard the strong, vibrant, cheerful voice of her aunt.

"This is Victoria Brand."

"This is Margo Brand," her niece said.

There was a short silence and then, "Margo? Margo!"

"Yes, it's me. I've returned to the land of my birth. And I must say it staggers me. What happened?"

"What d'you mean?"

"It's unrecognizable."

"Oh, you're talking about *Manhattan*," Victoria said. "As to that, I wouldn't know, you couldn't get me there under *any* kind of duress. *Here*, where I live, it's the same as always. I shall expect you tomorrow."

"Nothing I'd like better; however—"

"You just get out of that miserable Sodom and Gomorrah and *come*. Why, Margo, this is such a surprise! I had your last letter, I didn't expect to see you until Fall. That was what you said."

"I changed my mind. My course was finished, and I thought I'd better get it over with; coming home, I mean. I knew it would be difficult, not to say traumatic, and it is. Anyway. I'll do a bit of looking around for a flat, and tap some resources for a job. Let's say I'll be up sometime next week, okay?"

"My dear child, you have wealthy parents, why kill yourself?"

"Have to stand on my own feet sometime."

"After all, you're only nineteen."

"No, I'm twenty-one."

"You're to be here tomorrow, and that's an order."

"I'd love to, but give me a week, please. It's compulsive, perhaps, but I yearn to find a place to live, and show my folio to some studios. Let's say I'll be in Cranford in a week or ten days; how's that?"

"Well, you seem to have become a strong-willed young person."

"I've had to. I love you, Aunt Vick, I can't wait to see you, and in the meantime wish me luck. I know you do, but say it, won't you?"

"I wish you luck," her aunt said dutifully. "Where are you staying, for heaven's sake?"

"At a hotel. All very comfy and pleasant."

"You're too young to be—"

"I was never young," Margo said lightly. "But let it go. Don't worry, I've my wits about me, and I'll take the town by storm. Just fix up my old room, so that I can be thinking about it, and I'll see you soon, my dear darling. I'll buy a little second-hand car and when I get there I'll take you for long drives. We'll have Lucullan lunches at country inns. Do you suppose you'll recognize me?"

"I'd know those violet eyes anywhere," her aunt said rather huskily, and they said good-bye, after which Margo sat at the window, feeling much better. *Now that I've talked to her,* she thought. *That wonderful woman who had never married, never given life to a child, never known the protection of a man, and who yet had done so much for so many unfortunates. If ever anyone deserved canonization it was Victoria Brand. She was unrenowned, a simple countrywoman, but in the secret annals of mankind her name would be written in shining gold, emblazoned forever on the screen of God's truth.*

• • •

There were plenty of three-hundred-dollar apartments to be had; it was Margo's intention to find one for about a hundred and sixty. "I'm afraid we have nothing to offer in that price range," various agents said regretfully. "Perhaps in Astoria or Jackson Heights."

"Oh no, it has to be in Manhattan."

She took her folio to this studio and that one. The comments were flattering. "You'll hear from us," she was told. "Things will be opening up in the autumn."

"But I need a job now."

"The summer is always a bad time."

She cabled her parents. NEED FUNDS, JOB NOT EASY TO FIND.

Four days later there was a check for three thousand dollars. "This should see you through," was the accompanying message. "Daddy and I accomplishing much. Love from us both."

She went to a second-hand dealer and bought a small, peach-colored Impala. At the hotel desk she squared her bill, loaded her bags in the trunk and back seat, tipped the porter who had helped her, and drove off. *I accomplished nothing,* she told herself, angry and disgusted. All she had done was wear out shoe leather. *What did less fortunate people do?* She stopped off for bacon and eggs at a Howard Johnsons, then got in the car again. A bee buzzed in the rear seat of the car. She slapped at it, and cut into the Hutchison River Parkway.

Her destination was just short of two hundred miles. It was a leisurely drive, the day sunny, with a rare blue sky and a gentle breeze coming in through the car windows. At Poughkeepsie she found a parking place, had a hamburger and a beer and then, about twenty-odd miles from Cranford, went into a joint and ordered a martini.

She sat there drinking, remembering all sorts of things, remembering Switzerland and the French Riviera, and Cannes, and the Haute Savoie and a little *ciudad* in Spain, where she had her first real love affair. Jose had been dashing and assertive, had been her chauffeur on a trip through Andalusia. Quick, fleeting... but memorable. *"I won't forget you, Senorita."*

"Nor I you, Jose."

At the Seville airport he had brought her flowers. *"Must you go?"* *he had asked, and she smiled and said,*

"Thank you, how wonderful it was to know you, amigo."

And then, presumably, he had found some other American girl to dazzle with his dark, velvety eyes, but she hadn't begrudged him, not for a moment. He had given her what she had needed at the time; it was enough. *I've lived, you know, a rather unusual life,* she thought, and remembered one evening in Granada. They had gone to a small outdoor cafe, sipped Sangria and cracked lobsters, and on the way back to her hotel, the Fenix, he had kissed her in a quiet back street. *"Yo te amo,"* Jose had said, and it had led to more serious things. She would never forget him, but then she would never forget many things: the Lac Leman, the Seine and the Loire, the Gaudi houses in Barcelona, and the Cathedral at Nantes. Her mind traveled back to Arles, in the Midi of France, with the antique shops, the butter-colored pottery on shelves, and the Piazza Grande in Venice, the canals of Amsterdam.

But you had to come home some time.

Even if it hurt, even if it hurt.

The waiter saw that her drink was gone. He came over and asked if she wanted another, and perhaps some antipasto? "I'm really not hungry," she said, but he smiled encouragingly at her, said she was too thin and should eat, and came back a few minutes later with a glorious plate of anchovies and tomatoes and red peppers and artichoke hearts. Fringed celery stalks, very fancy, and carrot sticks and radishes made into little flowers.

"You must eat," he said solicitously. "Put some meat on those bones, you're too thin, young lady."

"It does look good," she said, and forked it up, while he stayed on and talked.

"You are from New York City?"

"Only recently."

"Ah?"

"I've lived abroad for quite a few years, I've just come back."

"Abroad?" he asked eagerly. "In Italy, perhaps?"

"Yes, Italy too."

"Where in Italy?"

"Florence, Rome, Amalfi, Napoli, Palermo…just about—"

"Palermo? I was born there!"

"Were you, really."

"Yes, beautiful, *si?*"

"Very beautiful."

"I go back to visit some day."

"You'll love it, I did."

"Tell me," he said, leaning forward.

"Italy is wonderful."

"Then this year maybe I go back," he said fervently. "I have family there. Good people, simple people. You liked it, you say?"

"Oh yes, very, very much."

"My partner, he's not here now, but he is Neopolitan. You were in Napoli?"

"For ten days. A bewitching city."

"I'll tell him. What hotel?" he asked, briskly.

"At the top of the hill, Parker's. All Naples was spread at my feet."

He rolled his eyes. "I too know Napoli. There was a girl there. I'll tell Rudi you were there. My wife and I met at La Spezia, on a holiday. You went there?"

"No, not there. Tell me about it."

"*Bella, bella.* Overlooking the town is the medieval castle of San Giorgio. We were staying at the Piazzo San Giorgio, a second class hotel, but very pretty, very nice. Our mothers were with us, we eyed each other in the dining room, and soon we spoke. The match was approved. She is Sicilian too. We walked out together, the rest following us, pretending to be looking for field flowers, very funny it was. The first time we kissed was on our marriage day. She had a body like a rose, small, delicate, very beautiful. Now we're not young, but I can't forget. Maybe we go back this year, maybe next year. Anyway, some time. Very expensive, I'm afraid?"

"Not all that much."

"And much sun," he said wistfully. "Here fog and rain, a really lousy climate, you agree? No real summer, no glorious sun. What are you doing here, if you spent years over there, *Signorina?* Why did you leave? To come back *here?*"

"This is home," she said simply. "I had a European education, and now I've come home."

"Imagine it," he said admiringly. "You left all that beauty and came back. Said good-bye to the sun and came back. Where are you going, *Signorina?*"

She said Cranford, it was just a dot on the map, about twenty miles or so from here.

"I know it," he told her. "There was a summer camp there. For the kids. It's gone now, but it was nice, all those years ago."

"I remember it," she said, and told him that she had lived in Cranford as a child, that she had a relative there.

"My Aunt Victoria," she said.

He stood by her chair. "You don't mean Miss Victoria Brand?" he asked.

"Yes. Yes, that's right."

"That big old house?"

"It's a very large house; you know it, then? The Brand House. I'm Margo Brand."

"Are you?" he said, and sat down, playing with a toothpick. There was an odd look on his face. He hesitated, and then said, "So you're a relation of the lady who died?"

"Who *what?*" She stared at him.

He put the toothpick in his mouth and chewed on it. "The reason I know so much about it, my sister used to teach school in Milletsville, about nine miles from Cranford. Your aunt was a trustee of the school. Everyone thought a lot about her. I know when my sister saw the notice in the paper last week she was quite upset." He went on slowly and deliberately, looking closely at her. "I understand she was a fine woman."

Margo put her glass down on the table. "*Was?*" she asked incredulously. "What notice are you talking about?"

There was a brief silence. Then he said, shrugging his shoulders as if in apology, "The death notice, the obit."

For a moment she felt faint. It was like an incredible dream. Then she rallied. "Are you telling me my Aunt Vicky is dead?"

she asked quietly and he said yes, he thought it was Tuesday. She picked up her drink and looked at it, then put it down again. She saw his eyes: he knew he had just delivered a bombshell.

"You're okay?" he asked anxiously, and she said yes, thank you, and he refused to charge her for what she had eaten and drunk. *"Libero,"* he told her, waving a decisive hand. *"Buona fortuna, Signorina."*

At the door he kissed her hand, and she got into the car again. Trying not to think, she drove the miles. That waiter…was it really true, or was she simply dreaming? "You're to be here tomorrow," Aunt Vicky had said…how many days ago?

There must be some mistake. She would drive up the path to the house and Aunt Vicky would come across the lawn and scold her. "Whatever *took* you so long?"

The sky had turned slatey and, an hour ago, with mackerel clouds scudding swiftly, the day had darkened. Now the downpour started, first just a few fat drops and then, like a cloudburst, an inundation. The trees bowed in the wind and the road was slippery. The windshield wipers swished back and forth, the car became steamy in the summer heat. She missed the turn-off at Roundsville, had to go back. *I need this like a hole in the head*, she thought, tightly, and then saw the tiny Main Street of Cranford just up ahead.

It really got to her then. Cranford meant a woman who had been everything to her in her formative years. If that woman was really dead nothing would ever be the same again. These familiar shops and stores: Elliott's Pharmacy, where they called her Margie, where for as long as she could remember, Bennie the soda clerk had brazenly dropped in two scoops for the price of one. The Post Office, where Sam Clive had instructed her in local history. The newspaper building, modest and one-storied, where Cletus Brown had given her her first smell of printer's ink.

She passed through the miniscule village and headed for Horseneck Lane, at the top of which the great old mansion stood high on a hill. And at that moment the heavens opened. There were now sheets of rain, so torrential that it was impossible to navigate a car. There was nothing to do but stop and wait, mopping her damp forehead. The rain came down in a blinding sheet, and she lit a cigarette, half out of her mind. Why must she sit here and *wait*…must *everything* go against her? So near and yet so far …

She drummed her fingers on the dashboard. "Will you stop this damned, infernal *rain?*" she cried, and ground her cigarette out in the tray. "I do not choose to be a prisoner, sitting here waiting, waiting.

"I do not choose …" she said viciously, and at a break in the downpour drove on again. A quarter of a mile later she was at the entrance to the estate. From here one could see the house, outlined against the sky, standing like a fortress, surrounded by its tall pines. There was nothing else on that hill, only that great old house, red Georgian brick.

It was a spectacular sight, awesome really. It could be a beautiful sight, when the sun hit the soft pink-red brick, the slender, shuttered windows, the three jutting dormers below the mansard roof and the two high chimneys at either end.

Or it could seem forbidding, as it did today, standing alone in the lashing rain, its brick turned the color of clotted blood. It was the first time Margo had thought of it in those terms but, staring up, she wanted to turn around and leave it in the distance. Because it seemed, suddenly, empty and forsaken, a ghost house. Dominating the landscape, it looked cruel and hard, timeless and impersonal, wicked, even. It seemed to say that no matter what person died and left its old walls, that was of no import, that time and tide made no mark on it, that it belonged to the ages and would stand, outlined against the sky, forever.

I don't want to go in there, Margo thought, chilled. She didn't want to drive the short distance left and go inside. She had never thought of it as a heartless house, but she did now. She cut the motor and stared. The great portico, with its Ionic columns, was severe and classic, and in this driving rain it was almost impossible to picture people strolling back and forth on the stone veranda, women in silken dresses and the scent of gardenia and *muguet des bois*, or men in smart morning clothes with spanking white ascots. Summer parties, and gardens adorned with Japanese lanterns, voices laughing.

There had been all that, but it was as if her imagination only led her to believe it. The rain swept over the green grass and the trees bowed in the wind. The house was dead, she decided, just a cold, elegant stone edifice without a heart. It belonged to history and to the ages, was almost as old as the country itself. She heard her aunt's voice.

"A band of English pioneers in 1659, following the lordly Hudson upstream in search of fertile lands, paused when they reached a place where the river seemed to linger to embrace the Sterling intervale. One of these men was an ancestor of mine, William Gaylord Brand, and upon this site he erected a small farmhouse and barn. It was more than fifteen years later that, prospering, he started to build the present house, Brand Manor, and in the year 1674 installed his wife, his sons and daughters and his household pets in this lovely Georgian home. In the family archives is a "true copy" of his will in his fine copperplate hand: *I do make and ordain my eldest son Aaron and my youngest son Noah to be sole Executors of my last Will and Testament, confiding in their faithfulness, and desiring them and all the rest of my Loving Children to study Peace and Live in Love and Unity, and the God of Peace be with you.*"

That tall, handsome woman, leading the way as she showed paying members of the New York State Historical Society through the house. "This cherry highboy was brought from Salem by Abigail Summers as part of her dowry. Note the Queen Anne legs. The portraits on the left of the hall are of Lucinda Phelps, from Greenfield, the bride of Nathaniel Brand, and the young son of that issue, James Lincoln Brand, my father."

There was a flash of lightning, a roll of thunder, and then the heavens opened again. The house itself was obscured by the storm. Putting the car into gear again Margo zoomed up the graveled driveway, squinting against the rain, and parked just outside the columned veranda. As she climbed out of the little Impala a jagged streak of lightning yellowed the sky, and the old house stood out in bold relief, beautiful, stern, wonderfully proportioned, graceful in its stark setting, as impregnable as any citadel. She dashed across the lawn and up the stone steps, shaking herself as she reached the entrance door, with its exquisite fanlight. Trembling, she stood there, unwilling to press the bell. Unwilling …

Because the hand which opened that door would not, could not be the hand of Victoria Brand. That hand was stilled forever. Margo would never lay eyes on that sweet face again, or rest her head on that comforting shoulder, or confide in that listening ear.

She's dead, Margo thought, *she's dead. I can't believe it, but she's dead.* There was an apocalyptic crash of thunder and she quickly put her hand on the doorbell. *I was too late*, she thought, despairing. *While I was house-hunting and looking for a job, Aunt Vicky died.*

And she would never forgive herself.

Too little and too late.

CHAPTER TWO

The person who answered her ring was Pompey, her aunt's butler, houseman, chief cook, and bottle washer. "So it's you at last," he said, trying for a cheery smile. "Some day, ain't it? Come in quick, come in and dry off."

"Pompey, is it true?"

"You heard about it?"

"I stopped off at Dalton for a drink. The owner of the place said—"

"She died last Tuesday, Miss Margo. We tried to get ahold of you, didn't know where you were, though."

"I'm glad *you* didn't have to tell me," she said. "You must have been dreading that."

"Was I *ever*," he said. "First thing I thought of every morning… how'm I going to tell that girl?" He shook his head. "Pictured you flying in here, all smiles and laughing and calling for her, 'Where are you, Aunt Vicky, I'm here …' " He cleared his throat and yanked open the door. "I'll get your bags and then fix you a drink."

"I'll help you with the bags."

"You ain't going out in that rain again." He spanked her lightly on her bottom and dashed out. She stood in the airy, gracious entrance hall, every detail of which was drawn indelibly on her mind…the maple chests, golden in color even on this dark day, flanking the two opposite walls, the portraits of Brand ancestors, the Georgian mirror and the bull's-eye mirror, the delicate little Queen Anne table with a pewter tray for calling cards.

The central staircase, an unusual feature for a house of this period, had forty steps due to the height of the ceilings on the ground floor. She used to slide down one banister and then the other, saying, "Geronimo!"

She was alone and unheard, and she whispered what Pompey had pictured her calling out, what indeed she would have called out if she hadn't stopped off in Dalton for that drink, if she hadn't heard the news beforehand.

"I'm here, Aunt Vicky, I'm here. Where are you, I'm here …"

But there was no answering voice. There was no sound at all except for that of the door banging shut as the wind caught it, and Pompey kicking at it to be let in. He was soaked to the skin, his shirt clinging to his chest. "Whew," he said, dropping the bags. "This beats all, this rain today."

He wiped his streaming head with a handkerchief. "Now I make us a drink."

"Take your shirt off," she ordered. "I'm of age, don't worry about me. Get that wet thing off you."

"Nothing much to see anyway," he said, shedding the dripping garment. "An old man's body."

"You've scarcely changed at all," she protested, and it was true. He was lean and fit, no protruding belly, and his hair had been gray when she had last seen him. It was still threaded with black. He was a strong, tall man who had worked hard all his life, the son of a man whose father had been a slave. He was a magnificent old man. They sat and drank, close to each other on a camel-back sofa. He had been liberal with the gin: the drinks were potent, therapeutic. She began to relax, actually heard her own released sigh. "Feeling better?" Pompey asked, watching her face.

"Yes, quite a bit better."

"Still can't believe it, can you? Me neither. I wake up and think, Pompey, you're an old guy, you must be dreaming things. I imagine I have a nightmare. And then I pinch myself and it hurts, so I know I ain't dreaming. She's gone. And me? I ain't got nowhere to go, Miss Margo."

"But she did leave you money?" Margo asked anxiously.

"Yes, enough for the few years I got to go. Besides some savings. It's just…this is where I been living for thirty years. It's home."

"I know." She put a hand on his knee. "What about John?"

"Broke up. Oh, sure. Anyway, he's doing well, working for Jim Bach, the lawyer man. Jim's old, Johnnie'll take over when Jim meets his Maker. No need to worry, he's up and coming."

"Douglas?"

"Farming. Different as night from day. 'Cept for their looks, not like twins at all. Different peas from the same pod."

She thought back. The twin boys had been ten when their mother died. The father, a farmer, had turned to drink. His liver had finally taken him off and then Victoria Brand had brought them into her home. Never married, childless, she had reared them, sent John to law school and Doug to agricultural college. When Doug graduated, she'd bought a parcel of land for him, but John lived on in the house.

Once, years ago, they had been like a family. Every June until September, they had lived together like siblings, spent day after golden day together. The twins were five years older than herself; she had thought them very grand and grown-up. And Pompey was right, they had been of disparate temperaments. John, his nose in a book, Doug the "wild" one, always getting into scrapes.

Those long, magical summers …

Cut short when she had been sent abroad for study. She hadn't kept a diary, like many of the other girls. She had, instead, written regularly to Aunt Vicky, as had her aunt to her, so that although they had been separated by the miles, each knew the most minute details and particulars of the other's life. Victoria Brand had been the *eminence grise* for a lonely young girl, her advice and counsel taking the place of a family situation. To her parents, she had dashed off charming, witty little notes and *billets*, but to Victoria Brand she had bared her very soul.

"If I could have seen her just once more," she said, and choked up.

"She sure did love you, that's for certain," Pompey said, putting his arm around her. "She saved all your letters, all of them letters are lying there in the eskritor in her room."

The little escritoire, a museum piece in itself, dainty, finely-wrought, with the funny little secret drawer that had so fascinated her. There her aunt had sat down, in her crisp, businesslike fashion, and written her letters to Switzerland. *Dear Margo …*

All those lost years.

"She didn't suffer, did she, Pompey?"

"Went quick, just like that. Don't think about it, because she must of went real quick."

"Her heart?"

"Seems like. She was getting on, after all. We'll talk about it another time. I'll take you upstairs to your room now, your old room. Maybe you want a nap, get some rest, how about that, dearie?"

"I won't go up yet. You want to start dinner, don't you? I'll help with it. I'll make a salad, and I can do a very good dressing for it. I just don't want to go up yet."

"Best way to take something in stride, keep yourself busy," he agreed. "Let's go in the kitchen and start the fixings."

• • •

They gossiped, the rain a counterpoint to their voices. Pompey insisted on being filled in on her schooling and life abroad. In "Yurrup," as he termed it. "Was the girls nice?"

"Some of them. It was a rather snobby school, you understand. However, the academic standing was high, you can generally count on European schools for that. When I graduated, I went to Paris and studied photography under a pupil of Cartier-Bresson's.

I have samples of my work, and the *atelier* where I studied in Paris will give me entree to some reputable galleries here. I was trying to find work, and an apartment when…when she died. I'd called her saying I'd be here this week. She sounded hale and hearty, she sounded her old self. Oh, if only I'd come right away …"

"Could be just as well," he said. "Not to see her like that. You remember her the way she always was, not like that."

"Not like what?" she asked, sharply.

He gave her a side glance. "Nothing…just better to remember a person at their best."

"You said she didn't suffer."

"Went quick," he said again, and stood by her chair admiring her salad. "Beautiful," he enthused. "Eyecatching, just beautiful."

It was a Salade Niçoise. She had raked the supplies for anchovy fillets, croutons, herbs and seasonings, had curled onion slices into pretty shapes, hard-boiled three eggs. "It does look nice," she said contentedly, and got up to start on the dressing for it. Pompey started singing a hymn, *Rock of Ages*, and she took the second part. They finished that and then sang *From India's Coral Strands*. The already bleak day darkened further and the kitchen clock said four and the pork roast sizzled in the oven.

Like always, Margo thought. Except for one thing. Aunt Vicky would not appear for dinner, there would be that vacant chair, and nothing would ever be the same again. Victoria Brand was dead, dead and buried, and a once dear face was never to be seen again. The reality of it penetrated at last, and the pain was so acute that she felt faint, and then there was the sound of the front door opening and closing.

And a voice.

"It's me."

"Mr. John," Pompey said matter of factly, and the footsteps came closer and he was standing there, someone she hadn't seen for thirteen years. He came into the kitchen, rain-wet but looking unwilted in a summer-weight suit, tie impeccable.

She went over to him and he put his arms around her. "I came home early, soon as I found out you were here."

"How did you know I was here, John?"

"How could I help it? You were spotted all along the line. Margo's here, I was told."

"Oh, come on, John."

"All right, then. Pompey phoned me. Said you were damper than a wet hen and prettier than ever."

"And you came home early. How nice of you, John."

He stood off and looked at her. "Is this really that little girl?"

"Is this really that little boy?"

Remembering, remembering...the twins, all lithe, long legs and wiry bodies, beautifully shaped heads, tanned, firm skin and handsome features. "Almost *pretty*," Aunt Vicky used to say. "With all that dark, gypsy hair ..."

They *had* looked like gypsies. Wild and free and untamed. It was how she remembered them, and she had to smile, for John was anything but gypsy-looking now. He was the complete young attorney, tall and lean and immaculate, very sure of himself, easy in his manner, authoritative. For one fleeting moment she was able to isolate his head from the rest of him, and see once again the reckless, daring face of the young John, like that of a street Arab in some Renaissance painting...and then the vision vanished. He was once more the John Michaels of today.

"I'm so glad to see you," she said.

"And I you. It must have been a great shock, Margo."

"I was just so unprepared."

"I wasn't. Just the same it doesn't hurt any the less."

"I know, I know."

"I'll make drinks," he said. "Come along."

"Wonderful."

They went into the living room, where John switched on a few lamps because, he said, "It's such a dark day, maybe this will help a bit. Gin's all right?"

"Yes, fine, Pompey made me a martini earlier."

"Olive, twist or onion?"

"Twist, please."

He made the pitcher of drinks and filled two glasses. "As for me, I go for olives," he confessed, and handed her her glass. "Too dry, Margo?"

"No, just right. I'm glad you're here, John, cheers to us both. How's Mr. Bach?"

"Just fine. Pompous as ever, but underneath a dry sense of humor and fine character. He's terrific to work with. He's not your average small-town attorney, he's got a first-rate brain, and he knows *law*. I couldn't have asked for a better mentor."

"I used to be afraid of him."

"So was I."

"With those *pince-nez* and the black cord dangling from them. And that voice way down in the cellar."

"Not to mention the bone-crushing handshake."

"Oh yes, that too."

"Tell me about yourself, Margo. About your life abroad; I'd really like to hear about that."

"Well, it was…years in school, you know, and—"

"And growing up."

"And growing up." She smiled across at him. "In the meantime, you did too. And now here we are, adults, drinking martinis together."

"And me wanting some liquid refreshment," Pompey said, strolling in.

"I thought you were slaving over a hot stove."

"Everything's under control, Mr. John."

"What's wrong with the cooking sherry?"

"Now you just pour me one of those, young man."

He took a swallow of the drink John handed him and leaned back. "Nice to see you two together," he remarked. "Been a lot of years, and a lot of water under the bridge. I can't get over you being so tall, Miss Margo. You were always such a little thing, like a canary."

"Oh, Pomp, your memory's gone back on you," John laughed. "She was a great, strapping girl and she ate like a hog."

"I can't remember what I was like," she said, and they sat there talking quietly until Pompey caught sight of the clock on the mantel, and sprang up.

"Got to shuck that corn now," he said, and started issuing orders. "Mr. John, you take your shower, get all clean and refreshed, and Miss Margo, I'll take your bags up now."

"I'll do that," John said. "Come on, Margo, you'll want to wash up too. We'll have another drink when we come down. Pompey, keep your eye on that roast, it smells damned good."

"Slaughter in the pan," Pompey announced. "Pork chops and apple slices and little potatoes."

"That sounds like something to look forward to," John said, and led Margo up the lovely stairway, with its bull's-eye newel posts and exquisite spool carving on the verticals. "I'm directly over you on the top floor," he told her. "I'll try not to thump about with my big feet. Doug always says I dig my heels in when I walk. There's a telephone on the landing right outside your room."

He pointed it out, on top of a small table over which hung a framed sampler done by a child of another century: GOD BLESS OUR HOME. "I have my own number," he explained. "A lawyer is like a doctor, calls frequent and sometimes very late at night. I couldn't inflict that on Aunt Vick."

He held her hand for a moment and then released it.

"Well, Margo," he said quietly, "it's been a long time, and I'm sorry you had to come back, after all this time, to—"

He didn't finish. Simply lugged her bags inside her room, patted her shoulder, and went to the door. Just outside he turned.

"It's changed all our lives," he said. "You must know that. Nothing will ever be the same again."

He closed the door and she stood there uncertainly, glancing vacantly around her "old room," with its tester bed, walnut *armoire*, chest on chest, lowboy and *semainier*, and all the rickety little Hepplewhite chairs, and the prints on the walls, and the great mirror topped by the American eagle, and the twin lamps made out of cobble-glass, and the daisy wallpaper old and faded. The same wallpaper…nothing had changed, not even the wallpaper.

She stood there, looking out at the rain-drenched twilight.

So it was true, Aunt Vicky was really dead.

CHAPTER THREE

When she went downstairs again, after changing, there was someone in the living room. A girl sitting on one of the sofas, leafing through a magazine. She saw Margo, threw down the magazine, and stood up.

"Do you remember me?" she asked.

"I'm embarrassed," Margo confessed. "I don't seem to—"

"Norma Calvet."

Again the past. The mousy little girl from the wrong side of the tracks. An absentee father and a mother who whiled away lonely hours in cheap bars. Norma Calvet …

The mousy little girl was mousy no longer. She was, in fact, breathtaking. She had height, a willowy body, eyes like jewels. She was wearing a simple banlon dress, tied at the waist, and her long legs ended in sandals that showed off lovely, tanned feet with curved toes and lacquered nails.

Doug and John and Margo and Norma…all those summers ago. *We smelled like children then*, Margo thought, *dusty and sweaty and faded blue jeans the worse for wear and the soles of our feet black from the dust of country roads …*

And now we're women, perfume-scented …

"Norma, it's such a pleasure," she said, and meant it wholeheartedly. "How wonderful of you to drop over."

"As soon as I heard you were here. Margo, darling, I'm so terribly sorry about your aunt. I had become such good friends with her. I can imagine how you feel. And John. She was like a mother to him. Margo, I just want to say that I did everything I could. I read to her, and bought her those cocoanut candies she liked so much. She was always so kind to me. My childhood wasn't very pleasant, and she was always so kind to me."

"She was kind to everyone in her orbit," Margo said. "She was a very unusual woman."

"John's taking it like a man, but I know it's a frightful adjustment. Poor boy, his eyes are so sad."

And Margo, assessing, thought, *There's something between them, Norma and John. Well, why not? She's very lovely-looking.* "You'll stay for dinner, won't you?" she said.

"Thanks, Margo, I was hoping you'd ask."

Why, she's become charming, Margo thought. *Manners like a duchess, if you please. And a frank, engaging twinkle in her eyes.* She remembered the forlorn little girl with the upstate twang. No longer the twang: her speech was perfect.

"What are you doing these days?" she asked.

"I work for Mr. Bach, I'm his secretary. My dear, I could tell you some stories…the things people tell their lawyers! Things they wouldn't tell their best friend." She laughed infectiously. "You know…up state author rips lid off staid old country town. Rape, incest, you name it. Get me drunk enough some day and I'll give you the low-down."

"Naming names too?"

"Have to get me *very* drunk for that."

When John came down they were sitting on the sofa, tittering. "And then this *very* proper pillar of the Methodist church threw their infant son's potty at his wife, with the result that she was in the hospital a week with a mild concussion and three broken ribs and a fractured elbow, because he threw the potty a second time. She happens to be an ex-prostitute from Buffalo, though that's only known to our firm; if the Commonwealth knew there'd be *such* a scandal. Oh, here comes John; he'd have a fit if he knew I was divulging the secrets of our trade. Do let's be ladylike."

She crossed her legs elegantly and when John came into the room, was saying, "That school in Switzerland, was it very posh, my dear?"

"*Very.* Daughters from minor royal houses, and those of film actresses."

"Covered with money from top to toe."

"You betcha."

"Hello, girls," John said, looking well-washed and cool, in white pants and a striped blue shirt open at the throat. "Like old times, isn't it?"

Looking up, stunned, Margo could scarcely believe her ears. What a *heartless* remark…just like old times …

After all, it was anything *but* like old times. The guiding spirit of this house was gone. And, she thought wonderingly, John's eyes didn't look all that sad to *her.* If he was indeed grieving, as Norma had said, it didn't particularly show. He stood at the liquor cart, a hand dashing back his dark, thick hair, and filled glasses from the martini pitcher. There was a cigarette between his lips now; he squinted against the smoke and brought their glasses over, very much the man of the house. Leaning against the mantel, his drink in a well-kept hand, he was the epitome of a "gentleman at ease," Margo reflected, putting the phrase into quotes in her mind. Handsome, lean, composed, he stood there, and with a pleasant smile, said, "To you both."

"Even in fatigues you look elegant, John," Margo said. The words came out by themselves. She was aware that they had a tart tone.

"Compliment or criticism?" he asked, with the same pleasant smile.

"Compliment, of course."

"As for you," he said, "you'd look good in a gunny sack."

"Compliment or criticism, John?"

"Compliment, of course."

"Would you mind telling me I'd look good in a gunny sack?" Norma asked. "Just so my nose won't be out of joint."

"You'd look good in a gunny sack," he said dutifully.

"It loses something in the repetition," she said, grinning.

"Then let it be a lesson to you."

"You can't win with John," Norma asserted, and turning to Margo, said substantially what John had said earlier in the day. "Tell me about your life abroad. We're the stay at homes; you must have had multifold adventures."

"You must have had too," Margo objected. "We all have our adventures, it doesn't matter where they happen."

"I'm not sure about that," John said. "I've never been beyond the eastern seaboard. No time for travel. I hope there will be now."

Once more she scored against him, lifting her head suspiciously. Why would there be time now? Because Aunt Vicky was dead? She swallowed, gulping down her anger and bewilderment.

"That's plain silly," she cried. "European travel is far less expensive than American travel. Ask any European who comes here for a good time. They leave their shirts here. Whereas in Europe you can go first class everywhere and manage very well. What's keeping you, John?"

"Well, of course there was Aunt Vick, she hasn't been well for several years."

"It's so odd. I talked to her just last week and she sounded super."

"Oh, no," he said. "She's been failing for some time. Tell her, Norma."

"Yes, it's true," Norma agreed. "A very slow and very sad decline. She was frail this year, her face paper-white. The doctor said—"

Pompey poked his head in the door and said dinner was ready, come in before everything was burnt to a crisp.

They sat, in the candle-lit dining room, with Pompey alternately serving and eating along with them. There was no fuss or formality, and he had cooked a good dinner: the "slaughter in the pan" was a dish of fat, juicy pork chops, with the roast potatoes browned and bone-white at their centers, the gravy brown and buttery. The corn was small-kerneled and tender. Pompey sat and ate, cleared the table, brought out the caramel custard and coffee, and sat again.

"Everyone satisfied?" he asked, as they pushed back their dessert plates and lit cigarettes.

"You're the best cook in the world," Margo told him.

The candles lit their faces: John's fine-boned, handsome face, with the thick dark hair; Norma's pluperfect one, her eyes glittering; Pompey's like pale ebony. Rain still lashed against the windowpanes, but inside they were cozy and warm, the house sealing out the elements.

"Let's go on a picnic while you're here," Norma said. "The way we used to do. The lake, remember?"

"I remember."

Before life caught up with us, she thought. Lanky and uninhibited, trying to best each other in the water, turning copper under the strong rays of the sun. Playing catch, skipping stones, floating on their backs, splashing, screaming, the sun a bright globe in the sky.

And sometimes at night, giggling and aware of their misdemeanor, skinny-dipping. A quick glimpse of a boy's body ...

"Will Douglas come too?"

"I shall certainly see that he does," Norma said emphatically. "I'll phone him tomorrow."

And in spite of everything, perhaps because of the dinner wine flowing freely, and the candles, the good food and friendship, Victoria Brand's niece began to vibrate to the talk and the comfortable buzz of conversation. There was the feeling of *belonging* somewhere. She would plummet down again, once alone in her room, but right now she clung to the companionship of the moment.

So that when Pompey suggested that they get in the car and go to, "That new place that just opened up a couple of weeks ago, The Strawman, just over to Leeksville way, have a little nip and tell me what it's like;" she thought, *Why not?* It would delay the bedtime hour, the moment of truth;

Norma said, "Would you rather not, Margo?"

And John, "I do have to keep a clear head for tomorrow."

"I don't mean until three in the morning," Norma said impatiently. "I do just think Margo would as soon put off being alone. Oh, I never say anything *right!* I just meant—"

"It's all right, Norma," Margo said steadily. "And you do say things right. If it's all right with John, let's go to The Strawman. I'd like it, and thanks, Norma."

"I've found that in times of stress the best thing I can do is get myself so exhausted that I sleep like a stone," Norma said. "And the rain's let up a bit, for the moment, anyhow. I'll just get my jacket, and Margo, better bring a sweater."

• • •

The Strawman was some ten or twelve miles away. They drove along a dark road with the only illumination the misty moon and the headlights of John's car. The air smelled like wine, fresh, cool and scented with country fragrances, sedge, harebrush and the ripe fruit hanging from trees. The rain was steady but not driving as they passed gas stations with their cold blue lights, a tavern or two with juke boxes blaring stridently, and small farmhouses with the jagged sounds of dogs barking.

At last a gambrel-roofed inn, white clapboard with shiny black shutters and the glimmering red lights of candles inside. "Here we are," John said, and pulled the car into a driveway. The years rolled back and Margo remembered Polly Butts, when they had been young and raw and unsophisticated, a little cottage turned into an eatery, where one could sit and eat hot roast beef sandwiches with a sliver of dill pickle and sometimes cole slaw on the side. The four of them, getting money from somewhere and making it big for the evening, Doug and John and Margo and Norma.

In those days a dollar went a long way.

They got out in the cool, almost chill night and dashed in trying to beat the fattest rain drops. It was a pseudo-saltbox, Cape Cod style, with white lilac bushes framing the Dutch-blue front door and inside ceiling beams and walls stripped to the brick and a hooded fireplace at the farthest end, logs blazing merrily. Maple furniture and captain's chairs and waiters in cherry-red jackets like hunting coats.

"This *is* rather nice, isn't it?" Norma asked, when they were seated, a winking candle on their table.

"Yes it is," Margo said. "Thanks for suggesting it, Norma."

"It was Pompey's idea."

"But it was you who knew it would be exactly the right thing to do on this first…first difficult evening here."

"I just had a hunch that it would…that it was more or less what you needed," Norma said, and, toying with a muddler as their drinks were served, looked up almost shyly. "It's been a lot of years, Margo. But you came back. After all these years, you came back. And yet, I always knew you would."

. . .

It was just before midnight when they stopped off to drop Norma at her apartment on Rook Road. "I'm on the second story," she said, pointing. "It's a pretty little place, you must come visit soon. There's a sundeck at the back, that's where I get my tan."

She waved, standing at the door as they drove off. "What a beauty she's grown to be," Margo said.

"Yes, she's a good-looking girl."

"Always the euphemist," she said lightly.

"After all, the stranger sees things with a fresh eye."

"Is that a quote, John?"

"I think so, but let's not belabor it. Here we are, home again." He parked the car, leaned over to open her door, and they got out. The rain was only a bleak drip drip at the moment, and they crunched over the pebbles of the driveway, then quietly walked up the four stone steps to the porticoed veranda.

"You go on up," he said, after putting his key in the front door. "I'll turn out the lights and lock up."

"Well, all right."

"And Margo ..."

"Yes, John?"

"I'm sorry it had to be like this. I'm just terribly sorry. Sleep well, and try not to think. That's what I do, try not to think. Sometimes it works."

"Yes," she said.

She started up the stairs, turned when he called. "Margo?"

"Yes, what?"

He hesitated, swung the keys round and round, and then said gruffly, "Get a good night's sleep."

"Yes, all right, John," she said, and went on up to her room. She sat on the edge of the bed and heard the house being put to bed. Heard doors, from a distance, closing, heard shutters banging, heard the progress of John's footsteps up the stairs. Her eyes were heavy, as if weighted down with Greek coins, like the dead of old. Without any preparation at all, just getting into a nightgown, she pulled back the coverlet and crawled into bed.

The misty moon made her blink, but as Norma had said, if you tired yourself out, you didn't have the energy to think, you just closed your eyes and turned on your side, with a sigh and a moan, and drifted into darkness. You were too tired to think. You lay there like a side of beef, out of it, quite out of it, and when the telephone rang you tried to pull yourself together. The telephone was ringing so get up and answer it, but you were too sound asleep, and although it kept ringing, and you screwed up your face, angry and annoyed, still there was nothing you could do. You were just too weary, too unable to move even so much as a muscle, and after a while it stopped ringing and the next thing you knew it was morning.

CHAPTER FOUR

Damn it, it was still raining. The sky was leaden, the window-sill, when Margo got out of bed and went over, was damp, with little moist bubbles. It was nine o'clock, but seemed more like a pre-dawn hour. She stood looking out at the drenched grass and then crossed the room. Opening her door, she smelled the eggs, the bacon.

Pompey was making breakfast.

She quickly showered, got into a robe and walked the length of the great hall outside, with the portraits lined up, gilt-framed. Aunt Vicky saying, "This is Aunt Doheny, this one's Uncle Portius, isn't he snooty-loooking? These upstate families had stiff backbones, I doubt I'd have had much in common with them."

On good days this hall was flooded with sunlight, burnishing the chests and highboys and streaming through the windows at either end. Today it was bleak and somber, a house that smelled of the death of many generations. She went into her aunt's room, looked around, a finger stilling her trembling lips. Bentwood rocker, four-poster bed, stained glass, afghan, milk glass and tea-caddy lamps, horsehair sofa. Aunt Vicky, springing up from a nap. "What time is it, child? Still time enough for some croquet before dinner?"

In the kitchen Pompey raised his kinky gray head. "You smelt the bacon," he said triumphantly.

"Well yes, it got me up."

"I made the eggs sunny-side up, the way you like, and I didn't foul up on the bacon either. I remembered you like it burned black."

"You have total recall," she said, and sat down at the plank table covered with oilcloth. He brought the skillet over, dropped the scallopy eggs onto her plate and draped the charred bacon over it all. "Now you eat every bite of that," he ordered.

"How about you?" she asked, digging in.

"I eat with Mr. John every morning. What are you going to do with yourself on another rotten day?"

"Read *Little Women* and eat an apple. How's your sister, Pomp?"

"Clara? Fine. Comes in to clean, as always. Be here around eleven."

"I'll be happy to see her again."

"She too. Still thinks of you as a little girl."

"You do too, don't you?"

"Yes, honey. It's what you are. Me, I'm seventy-four. Hate to be hanging since I was your age."

"Pompey, sit down with me."

"Okay, honey." He poured himself some coffee.

"I'd like to hear about how it happened," she said quietly. "You can tell me now, I'm ready for it."

He said, "All right, Miss Margo," and draining his coffee cup, set it down in the saucer. "Like I said, it was last Tuesday. I have a few extra things to do, you know, work for some other families, here and there, and such like. Yes, and on that day it was my time to take the power mower on this here property, so around about three in the afternoon I came back here and called out to her, your aunt, and said what was going to do. Generally about that time of day she'd be in the garden, in that old Panama hat of hers, weeding around the flower beds, but when I got here she wasn't in sight and I didn't think much, I just did my work. Then, say at five or so, I went to the kitchen here for my drink. I like that Gatorade, and I was thirsty as could be. She wasn't here in the kitchen neither, and I begin to get this peculiar feeling that there was something not right, not in the ordinary run of things. The house, this house, it sounded so empty."

He coughed behind his hand. "I love this house, always have loved it, though some say it has a spook feeling to it. This is a house out of our history, colored and white, and it means the world to me. But more than that, she did. And on this day I'm talking about, there was a feeling to this house I didn't like. I was uneasy, and seeing shadows here and there, and somehow I felt sad and upset. Maybe it was more than that, because I marched up those stairs, no reason why, but I did. She was lying there in her room, on the bed. I saw her and I backed away, but Lord, I'm a man, ain't I? So I grit my teeth and walked up toward the bed. She was quiet, very quiet, and her eyes, they were half open. Looked to me like she suffocated, her face was all purple, and the coronor did say yes, she choked on her own excretions, meaning, when I asked him, she must have coughed up some and swallowed it and, no help handy, she just gave up the ghost."

He coughed again and made no effort to hide the tears that glittered in his eyes. "I'm sorry to have to tell you this, Miss Margo," he said. "Now you just eat up, you hear?"

She bent to her plate. "Yes, Pomp."

He got up and blew his nose, stood at the screen door, mastering himself. When he came back he was in control. "I got some things to do," he said matter of factly. "I gotta go."

"I'll see you later."

"You won't be alone for long; Clara be here in an hour or so."

She finished, did up her dishes, and left the kitchen. The rain was pounding down without letup. She roamed through the lower floor of the house, smelling the ancient damp, the past that filtered through from other centuries, other times. The rain ...

In Nice, one holiday on the French Riviera, she had bought an umbrella from a little shop. The price had been about eight francs or a dollar fifty. A sturdy little bumbershoot, under which she had walked the length and breadth of the Promenade des Anglais. In a small cafe, back in Beaulieu, the management had played, with broad smiles, an American record on the juke box, *Big, Bad John*. "Thanks so much," she had said, and had dashed out to the roadway for the bus to Monte Carlo.

So much of what she had done had been done alone, she thought. The Lido and the Estoril, lying in the sun, watching others hand in hand. She went upstairs and washed her hair, sat drying it with a Turkish towel. And then she went back to her aunt's room, as she had known all along she would.

She sat down at the little desk, the "eskritor" as Pompey called it, and pulled down its curved top. The feel of the old wood was like silk, satiny with age, and with a faint smell of verbena, her aunt's scent. It was at this desk that her aunt had conducted her daily business, written letters, signed checks, and from the view out of the windows, had looked onto her beloved gardens below.

She was a happy woman, Margo reminded herself; for as long as she lived she was happy. All those decades, and the changing seasons, the lovely security of this fine old house, and Pompey to do for her.

Think only of that, she bade herself, and opened the center drawer, where she found what Pompey had said she would find… letters, years and years of letters from a growing girl to an aging woman. Dear Aunt Vicky. Piles and piles of letters, tied neatly with blue ribbons, scattering as she untied the ribbons. Bits and pieces of her years in Switzerland stared up at her: "Some of the girls are nice, some quite dreadful. Like Lise Waldheim …"

Lise Waldheim! A beautiful girl, but hostile… "You think you are so wonderful, Margo? Just because you won the Seward medal?" *Was I ever this young*, she wondered, and read other letters, saw her development from child to young woman. "Dear Aunt Vicky, I'm staying at the Hotel Jules Cesar in Arles …"

Oh yes, that was a lovely place, she remembered, and read on. "It was once a monastery, with the eleventh century church of St. Trophime at its center. Mademoiselle Faust is our duenna. Do I like her? Perhaps I do, at odd and sundry times. She is very strict, and insists that we speak nothing but French on this little outing. She looks like a spider, has only half a stomach because of an operation. Today we went to Fontvielle, to see the windmills and in particular the one in which the author Daudet lived. We hired car and driver at Montmajour. The driver's name was Michel. He had light hair, as light as my own, and teased me in a nice way, and of course I fell rather in love with him, which I knew he sensed. There were plains that stretched golden under a cerulean sky, and then the windmills, their giant arms stilled forever, the peaked thatches of their roofs piercing the blue overhead. In front of Daudet's mill a tall, strong cypress stood guard. We toiled up the ascent in the burning sun, stumbling over the calciferous rocks, and then went inside to the dim cool of the mill's interior. It's a museum now, that mill which once housed one of the famed authors of the Provence, Alphonse Daudet."

Not bad for a fifteen-year-old, she thought, and skipped hastily through other letters from other years. "Dear Aunt Vicky: I am sitting at the Florian in the Piazza San Marco, with the pigeons wheeling overhead ..."

Who was that child, she thought, depressed. *I don't know that child, I was* never *that child!*

And then, in the enormous welter of her own letters, neatly bound as to year and tied with the blue silk ribbons, she found a singular thing and, finding it, became once again a little girl, learning about palindromes. "Something that reads backwards the same way it does forwards," Aunt Vicky had said. "*Subi dura a rudibus.* There are idiots who have spent a lifetime composing palindromes, but we must only feel pity for such misguided souls. It's simply an interesting semantic thing, and I only mention it in passing."

This palindrome, scrawled on a single sheet of yellow foolscap, was the classic of all palindromes. The writing was frenetic, slanting crazily, taking up most of the long page, and with an address to her, Margo.

Margo, take heed …

At the bottom of the page were three exclamation marks, digging heavily into the paper, so that in places the foolscap was torn through.

She looked long at it, held it upside down and sideways, and wondered anew. Among all these letters written by her young self, and neatly tied with sentimental blue ribbons, was this odd what have you, and was it supposed to mean something to her, and if so couldn't there have been something less mysterious?

A *palindrome?*

MADAM, I'M ADAM

And at the bottom, a spiky signature and a date.

Victoria Brand, June 9, 1973.

What could she have meant? Margo wondered. Yet she was sure it was some kind of message, some kind of communication from the dead to the living. Because it was the opinion of many medical minds that those who were doomed sensed their impending destruction, had a glimpse of the Dark Horseman, and spent their last days putting their house in order.

But what was one to make of this? It meant nothing to her, nothing. If a message, why not in plain English…she could have said, without equivocation, whatever she had meant to say.

Unless …

Unless she had wanted this weird communication to be disguised, oblique, of no import to anyone other than herself, Margo. What reason could there have been for that, then? Of whom was she suspicious, doubting? So that she must use a secret jargon—a code, really—to transmit something of value to the one person it was meant for …

She sat there, trying to puzzle it out.

MADAM, I'M ADAM

I haven't the faintest idea what it means, she thought, and bound the letters up again, once more in their blue silk ribbons, and then stuffed the palindrome into her pocket, to be mulled over at leisure. There was a reason for this eerie occultism, she told herself, and closing the desk, went out into the corridor again, where she heard the opening of the front door. Going to the staircase, she peered down.

"Who's there?"

"Miss Margo? It's me, Clara."

Gladdened, she ran down the stairs, flung herself into the arms of Pompey's sister. "There there," Clara said. "You're all alone? That's no good. Come on, we'll have a cup of coffee before I start my work. How are you, honey?"

"Very, very lonely."

"Can imagine, and Pompey too."

They sat at the kitchen table, drinking the perc coffee. "You're so young," Clara said. "Young enough to take things in stride. Not like Pomp, he's an old man. I could make room for him, but he won't hear of it. This here has always been his home. Poor fellow, he's almost out of his mind."

"Yes, I'm so concerned about him."

"Some little money for him, others as well. She used it almost all up, poor soul. What you're going to do with this house I don't know, Miss Margo. Taxes will eat everything up."

"What do you mean, what am I going to do with this house?"

"Oh, I shouldn't have said nothing. Don't say I said anything. I thought you knew. I thought—"

"Knew what?"

Clara looked worried, anxious, conscience-stricken. "They'll tell you," she said. "I just thought you knew."

"Tell me *what?*" Margo asked, urgently. "I won't say anything, I promise, Clara. Tell me what?"

"She left this house to you. I thought you knew that. I made a boo boo. You won't say I told?"

"She left this house to *me?*"

"You're her blood," Clara said.

"But after all …"

She sat there thinking about it. This great manor house, high atop a hill, filled with possessions from other centuries…*hers?* "Are you sure?" she asked Clara.

"But you won't let on I told?"

"No no, of course not!"

"It's yours, Miss Margo." Clara got up quickly. "Got to start my work now," she said, looking worried. "I didn't mean to speak out of turn."

"It's all right, Clara, don't think about it again."

When she was alone she poured herself another cup of coffee. She was dazed, unbelieving. How could she make this house her home? Her work had to be in some large, metropolitan area… how could she earn a living here? Why would Aunt Vicky make such a quixotic gesture? Why?

The vacuum cleaner hummed, vying with the sound of the rain. MADAM, I'M ADAM…*Dear Aunt Vicky, I am sitting here at a little cafe in Annecy…Dear Margo, the pear tree is in blossom, it's Spring again, wish you were here …*

Don't leave me, she thought pleadingly. *Don't leave me.*

But of course Aunt Vicky already had.

In her room she heard the sound of the doorbell. Clara called up. "Company," she said, her voice drifting up the stairwell.

It was Mr. James Huntington Bach, accompanied by a fresh-faced young man. The lawyer held out a liver-spotted hand and then brusquely kissed her. "I'm sure you know how sorry I am," he said, in his low-placed voice,

"Yes, of course, Mr. Bach."

He thrust his *pince-nez* on a fleshy nose. "I want you to meet Ed Corliss," he said. "One of our assistants. He'll be on the premises from this day forward. There's the inventory, you understand. Every single piece of historical value must be ticketed according to catalogue. I'm afraid it will be something of an inconvenience to you, Margo, but it has to be done."

"I don't mind."

They went into the living room. "I knew you were back in the country," the lawyer said. "Your aunt said you were due here shortly. When she was taken so suddenly I tried to reach you, but with no success. She said you were staying in some hotel, but none of us knew *what* hotel."

"It was the Plaza."

"Of course there was no way of knowing."

"Or any way of me knowing what was happening to her. If I'd had any idea she was failing, I'd have come right up."

"Failing? No no, nothing like that. She was herself right up to the end. As strong as an ox, seemingly. The end was quite unexpected."

"But John said—"

"She was one of the lucky ones. No wasting away, no foretaste of death. Right as rain one minute, dead as a doornail the next. That should make you feel better. She never had a bad day in her life." He pulled out a copy of the will, asking her to read it and then ask any questions she might want to raise. "In the meantime," he said, "could young Ed and I have a glass of Harvey's?"

"Oh, I didn't mean to neglect my duties as a hostess …"

"Stay seated, I know where the sherry's kept," he said, and pushing her down on the sofa again, went to the liquor cabinet and, opening it, brought out a bottle of Bristol Cream and filled three glasses.

"Ed…Margo …"

He placed a glass in front of each of them, lit a cigar, and then sat down and handed her the stiff-looking, legal document that was her aunt's will. The paper felt cold in her hands, cold and impersonal, a far cry from the chatty and gossipy letters she had received through the years. With a determined effort of will, she stilled the trembling of her hands and read the dictates of a woman no longer of this world, while Jim Bach and his assistant made a pretense of riffling through some papers of their own.

There were a few codicils and sub-codicils, but in the main it stated that she, Margo Brand, was to inherit the property known as Brand House, and the stipulations were thus:

To my grandniece, Margo Meredith Brand, flesh of my flesh and blood of my blood, I leave this four-acred property, with everything inside the house and outside it, providing that she take up residence in said house. If she does not wish to live under the roof of Brand Manor, and make her home within these walls, then the entire property, by default, is willed to the New York State Historical Society, free and clear, without lien or obligation of any nature. To my dear niece, I entrust this charge: that under no circumstance will this estate be divided, lessened or in any way mutilated, or the contents within the house sold or auctioned. I, Victoria Brand, honor and esteem the history of our nation and will wish, with my dying breath, to preserve the artifacts of its beginnings. That what has been, under God, shall remain intact and undisturbed, and that young minds and aspiring souls may see and touch and know what their honorable past has been, that they may be reminded of our humble pioneer origins and the toil of those who hacked their way through a wilderness.

The lawyer saw that it was difficult for her to speak. "Yes, it's very nice, isn't it?" he said, putting his cigar into an ashtray. "A few mixed metaphors, but otherwise…well, quite touching. Just the same, Margo, it's binding. It says, without the poetry, that the house is yours providing you decide to live in it. If not, then it reverts to the Historical Society of this state. So you have a decision to make. Either/or."

He held up a hand. "No need to be hasty," he said. "You just think about it. Nothing in this will says you have to make up your mind on the spot."

She said, "How could I possibly live here?"

"The house is in good repair."

"I don't mean that. Is there any money? I'm sorry, I have to ask it," she said. "Because to maintain a property like this is beyond my means. I haven't any means at all, as a matter of fact. You know that, Mr. Bach. I'm just starting out. I'll have a profession, but it means living in some large city."

"I can tell you right away," he said, "that there's no money at all. There are bequests to a number of persons, which the remaining capital covers. To you, Margo, simply the house and the land. You can't sell any of the furnishings, either, though even one of them would bring you a pretty penny. The will clearly stipulates that the house remains untouched."

He gave her a long look, shifted in his chair, and shrugged. "For some reason your aunt painted you into a corner. She was a very bright woman and she must have had her reasons."

He got up. "No hurry, as I said. Gather your wits about you and…no hurry at all. We'll be running along now. I hope Ed here doesn't get in your hair."

"I don't mind at all," she said mechanically, and they went off, umbrellas held up in the gusty rain. Sighing, she turned away and, alone, read the will again. The legatees were simple people, of no account in the great world outside. Pompey, John and Douglas, Clara, the postmistress, the mailman.

Small sums of money, and nothing left over. *Why, she was almost broke*, Margo thought, touched and haunted. Another few years and this will would have been meaningless as regards the persons mentioned. There would have been no assets to fulfill the obligations.

She went up to her room and lay down on the bed. The vacuum cleaner, now that the "company" was gone, hummed again. The rain dashed across the windows, swept the trees outside. Everything was dark and dreary. She was in a bedroom of a house that now belonged to her, but what did it mean? *If there was only a way*, she thought, tossing. Some way to keep her inheritance, live here.

That's just plain nonsense, she thought. A twenty-one-year-old girl managing a house like this? Why, she hadn't even voted yet!

You didn't look a gift horse in the mouth…but just the same what could Aunt Vicky have been thinking of?

• • •

Clara woke her out of a sound sleep, knocking at her door.

"Miss Margo?"

She struggled up and wiped sleep out of her eyes. "I just dropped off after they left," she explained.

"I'm finished with my work. I made some fresh coffee and a little cake. Come on down and I'll cut some for you."

"Oh, wonderful, Clara."

It was a buttery pound cake, and the coffee was hot and strong. They sat and chatted, and then Clara went off, in her shabby little heap, an old Chevy, and the house was silent again. She wandered through it: she had to come to some kind of decision, but she couldn't put her mind to it. *What shall I do with myself now?* she asked, staring out at the rain, and then the phone rang.

"It's Norma. How are you, Margo?"

"So so. How nice of you to call."

"You read the will."

"Yes, I read the will."

"I'm sorry the weather's so bad."

"So am I, it's getting me down. You'll come to dinner tonight?"

"Thanks much, I can't."

"Oh, I *am* sorry."

"John nixed it. You and he have to have a long talk."

"We do?"

"Yes, and he's right, Margo. After all, you know the terms of the will now. You'll have to come to some kind of decision."

"But what does that have to do with—"

"It's a family matter," Norma said, gently but firmly. "Once things are settled, it'll be different."

"But—"

"I hear my master's voice. Mr. Bach is looking for something. It's undoubtedly right under his nose, but he'll never find it. Men are really so helpless, aren't they? Keep your chin up. See you soon."

"Good-bye, Norma."

A few minutes out of a long, tiresome day.

And now what? she thought, her teeth on edge. But the phone rang again. She got it before it had a chance to ring twice. "Is this Margo?" a voice asked.

"Yes, who's this?"

"Douglas Michaels. Hello, honey."

"Douglas…oh, I'm so glad you called."

"I was apprised of the fact that you were in these parts," he drawled. "I guess you feel pretty rotten."

"Yes, very. The weather doesn't help, either."

"Isn't it a bugger."

"Just awful. I don't know what to *do* with myself."

"I wish I could say the same. I have a dozen things to take care of, but tomorrow's another day. How about driving out this way in the morning, when the weather will be better."

"The weather will be better?" she repeated, looking out the window.

"Yes, sunny and coolish. You remember where Peking Hill is, don't you?"

She said promptly, "About fifteen miles from here, just north of the turning at Corinth Road."

"Just beyond is my spread. Fourteen acres of good farmland. Come around eight, nine, ten, or eleven. I'll be waiting."

"All right, Doug. Unless this rain keeps up."

"Trust me. Tomorrow will be bright and shining. Do you still have those freckles?"

"A few on my nose."

"See you tomorrow. I'll give you lunch."

• • •

John arrived at just before six. He greeted her and asked to be excused while he got under the shower. She had changed into a long dress, a caftan, really. Pompey entered and looked at her approvingly.

"Will wonders never cease," he said, and wandered kitchenward. She had already made the salad and now sat smoking, restless, looking out onto the drenched trees and bushes, disoriented and jittery. *I could use some guidance*, she told herself. *What am I supposed to do?*

A fancy school in Switzerland never prepared me for this, she thought, and paced the floor, lighting another cigarette, and then abruptly sat down again. As if seeking some help from her dear departed aunt, she looked up at the ceiling. 'You must have had *some* plan," she said, aloud, and then heard John coming down the stairs.

He walked in and said now he felt more like a human being, and went to the liquor cart, making martinis without asking her. He busied himself, standing there with his back to her, a tall, dark-haired young man, and she suddenly realized something. *What about John? What about John, now the house had been left to her ...*

Why, this was John's home, had been his home from boyhood on. What was he going to do now?

She pondered the question, while he stirred rhythmically. *If she accepted the gift of the house, what would he do? And if she declined it, and the house went to the Historical Society, what would he do?*

It seemed John had a decision to make too, and she remembered what he had said as he put her bags down in her room.

"It's changed all our lives...you must realize nothing will ever be the same again ... "

He poured the drinks, walked over to her and handed her the frosted glass, then sat down in an easy chair. "Cheers," he said.

"Cheers to you. How was your day, John?"

"So so. And yours?"

"Rather wearing. This rain. Otherwise I'd have taken the car and driven some place."

"It will be better tomorrow."

"Who says?"

"The weather report. Rain ending tonight. So take heart." He crossed his legs and lit a cigarette. "Margo, I want to warn you," he said. "There will be people coming in and out of this place. You're in a peculiar position, you've inherited a property. This is a well-known house, a relic of another age, with a fantastic history. It belongs to you now. I'll try in every way possible to protect you from the merely curious, the sensation-seeking. Historians with good credentials will, naturally, have every right to view the premises. But I don't want you badgered. And you don't have to see anyone you don't want to. So just take each day as it comes, and if you're in doubt, let me know. Just—"

He hesitated, frowned, and then shrugged. "How's your drink?"

"Fine, thanks. Is this what it means to…to have something left to you?"

"Yes," he said. "Having something valuable left to you is a responsibility."

"You mean a white elephant," she said listlessly.

"That sounds, you know, rather unkind."

"I trust you to see beyond the harshness of the words."

"I do see beyond them."

"I just don't understand what it all means. And I feel, suddenly, without wisdom, without comprehension. I just feel that somebody should help me, I don't know who. I have this feeling of vertigo, as if I were standing on a high ledge, clinging to the safety of a solid foundation, and that the foundation is beginning to crumble. I feel frightened."

She clasped her hands. "I can't see her face," she said. "I try to see it, remember it, but I can't, John. It's all too much for me; I can't cope."

"So don't try to," he said. "Your teeth are chattering. Are you cold? Shall I make a fire?"

"No, don't bother, it's almost dinner time."

But he insisted. And it helped. The logs, apple-wood, blazed merrily as John poked at them. They stopped talking. This was the boy who had kissed her in the daisy field. Doug had kissed her too. The way children kissed, before they knew what kisses could be like. "I love you," he had said. Doug had told her the same thing. The rings they had made her, tiny colored beads strung on thin wire. "That's pretty, Margo," Aunt Vicky had said. And the bracelet, made out of corn silk. From John or Doug? She couldn't remember.

He's marvelous-looking, she thought grudgingly.

And again thought of a Renaissance portrait. Caravaggio. Dark head bent to the fire. Hair thick and dark and strong.

"Isn't that better?" he asked, throwing down the fire tongs.

"It's lovely, thank you."

"Drink up," he said, refilling her glass. "Well, hello, Pomp. Are you ready for us?"

"Dinner is served," Pompey said with mock solemnity. "Bring your drinks in with you."

• • •

She was in her room at a little before ten. She listened to the faint thud of John's footsteps above her. Doug was right: he did dig his heels in. But she welcomed the sound in the quiet house. She left her door open, and apparently so had John, because when she went out again, to walk back and forth in the corridor—restless and not at all sleepy—she heard the distant tap tap of a typewriter. He must be preparing some brief or other.

How proud Aunt Vicky must have been.

My godson, the lawyer …

She went back to her room and wrote a letter to her illustrious parents, now in Russia. "I've inherited Aunt Victoria's house. It's a Homeric joke, is it not? Tonight, talking to John, I called it a white elephant. How can I possibly—"

She tore the letter up. Made ready for bed, got in after she turned off the several lamps, lay listening to the wind and the rain. Above her the footsteps paced again. Listening, she followed their peregrinations. John was walking back and forth, back and forth. Why? Couldn't he sleep either?

I don't believe it will be a nice day tomorrow, she thought, and tensed as a thunderclap shattered the night. The sheets felt damp, and she bunched her pillow beneath her head.

And it finally came home to her in full force. The fact of the matter was that this house was *hers*. Aunt Victoria was dead, but she had left something behind, a great pile of stone and brick, and it now belonged to her, Margo. *It's too much to handle*, she told herself, and recalled all the houses, castles, mansions, stately homes she had seen in Europe. There they were, standing fast, while those who had slept in their beds and eaten at their tables and held court on their thrones had long gone. Mere mortals exist but briefly, whereas brick and mortar have longer endurances, and into whose magnificent rooms the curious stream, tourists looking for a thrill on holiday. "This is the bed in which King Louis XIV slept," the guides said. "Napoleon was made Emperor as he knelt on this slab of stone." "On this balcony King Victor Emmanuel …"

A mechanism in her brain turned off, like the flick of a radio dial, and thoughts stopped. Outside the rain continued, bending the great old trees, and it was midnight, dawn six hours away.

• • •

The telephone?

She looked over at the bedside clock. It was three in the morning. Just the same, the telephone was ringing. She sprang out of bed and, opening her door, went out to the hall. It was dark, and she had to grope her way. Then she felt the damp-cold instrument, picked up the receiver.

"Hello," she said, in the thick dark.

There was no answer.

She said again, "Hello. Hello?"

But there was no answer.

Someone had made a mistake. Or had she been dreaming?

She went back to her room again, climbed into bed. She must have been dreaming. A hand under her cheek and the covers pulled over her.

She must have been dreaming.

And then, like a pistol shot, the phone again.

She raised her head, listening. This time she wasn't dreaming. This time she was wide awake. And alert, wary. What ghastly news now? She hopped out of bed and raced outside to the phone.

"Yes, hello," she said, waiting.

There was no answer.

But there was something else. There was a sound, a very soft sound, but it was there. It was the sound of someone breathing.

Chilled, she listened, then said, "Who is this?"

There was no response. Only the quiet, eerie breathing.

"Who is it, who is it?" she cried.

There was only the breathing.

She held the receiver to her ear, listened attentively, and then quietly hung up. When she went back to her room there were goose-pimples on her skin, and she sat on the edge of the bed. Remembering. It had rung last night too. She had been too fagged out to register it more than subliminally, but yes, the telephone had rung late last night too.

She knew, of course. That it would come again. And it did. Five or ten minutes later. She sat and heard it out. Ring, ring, ring…and then she started counting. Eleven, twelve, thirteen …

And then it stopped.

It was half an hour before she got into bed again. By then the sky had imperceptibly lightened, and she was so groggy that the phone could have rung again but she wouldn't have known it. She fell into a deep, soporific sleep, accepting what had happened. The telephone late at night, two nights in a row. Once could have been a mistake. But twice?

Turning in her sleep she thought she heard it again, but this time it was probably, after all, a dream.

CHAPTER FIVE

The next morning was one of exquisite brilliance. Every blade of grass was diamond bright, birds sang and trilled, the sky was like a Wyeth painting. Margo couldn't help marveling at the beauty of the day, and in the kitchen she told Pompey about the telephone calls.

"Neither you nor John heard anything?"

"This is a big house," he reminded her.

"Who would do that?" she asked. "I certainly didn't expect, in this neck of the woods, one of those crank phone calls…you know the kind."

But she saw at once that he didn't, and explained. "Some pervert calls you at odd hours and either says nasty things or just breathes hard into the phone."

He was shocked and stern. "You don't mean it!"

"Well, that's why young women living alone have unlisted numbers. It's true in every large city in the world."

He muttered as he served her breakfast. "Like to show him a thing or two," he said angrily. "Just let me get a hold of him." Then he sat down, wonderingly.

"But up here, Miss Margo? I just can't credit it."

"I feel the same way," she said. "But it happened. Let's have another cup of coffee, Pompey, and then I'm going to drive out to Doug's place."

"That's the best idea I can think of," he said approvingly. "You'll be surprised what he's done with that farm."

And so she left a little before ten, drove through hilly country, recognizing this landmark and that one, then came to the mailbox in the road, with the flag up and the name MICHAELS in red lettering. There was a crossbar fencing, beyond which, through the trees, one glimpsed a hospitable-looking farmhouse in that lovely shade of barn-red, matching the barn itself. There was a silo, silvery in the sun, wheat waving in a field. She heard the chug of a tractor.

"Hi," a voice said, as she drove through the open gate, and he came out of the house, banging a screen door.

She waved out the car window. "Doug?"

"Yup."

"I'd have recognized you anywhere."

"Can't say the same for you," he said, looking her over. "You were just a skinny little kid."

"I got over it."

"You certainly did."

She looked into the eyes of John's identical twin. Smiling eyes, the same thick, dark hair, the same mouth and nose and chin. But there the resemblance ended, and she had to laugh, thinking of John's well-cut clothes, his impeccable striped shirts with French cuffs.

Douglas wore no shirt at all. He had on denim pants and that was that. His torso was strong and muscular, though not burly; hairy but not ape-like.

"You look like Heathcliff," she said.

He opened her car door. "Get out, you foreigner, step lively now."

"Hello, Doug," she said, stepping out on the grass.

"Hello, Margo. I'd have preferred seeing you again after all these years under different circumstances. Well, it can't be helped. Come on, I'll show you around."

In the scented meadow he introduced her to his heifers, Jenny, Phyllis, Marianne, and Lois. "They're good milkers, the little darlings. One of them's ready to calve, as you can see. I worry about her; she always has a difficult labor."

"Will it be soon?"

"Any time now."

There were goats, in an enclosure, horned and with split-pea eyes. Fowl: chickens, hens, a rooster. "My alarm clock," Douglas said. Two pigs, He and She, rolling in mud, and some romping dogs. Doug signaled, and the man on the tractor pulled to a stop.

"Remember little Margo?"

The man waved down.

"Shorty McLean, you worked for Doug's father," Margo cried.

"Sure did. Glad to see you again. Sorry about your aunt. Wonderful woman. Come 'round again, Miss Brand."

He revved the motor and went on. "Shorty McLean," Margo said, looking after him. "Oh, how the past comes back!"

"Yes," he agreed.

"I remember your father's farm. All run down and going to seed. I knew how you felt about it."

"I felt lousy about it," he admitted. "I made up my mind I'd have my own acres some day, and she made it come true. I loved that woman."

Abruptly, he said, "I read a lot of your letters, she let me. She used to laugh at me because I called you the princess with the golden hair. It was the way I thought of you. Only you kept going away, and then you went away for good. To that tony school in Switzerland."

"I did what I was told to do."

They went into the house, through a side door that led into a kitchen, with an enormous hearth over which hung a gigantic kettle. It appeared to be one of those houses that had started as one big room, and to which adjuncts had been added over the years. "Tell me about it, Douglas," she prompted.

He was only too glad to, and there was pride in his voice. "A Mr. Luther Pettiford owned it; it's a house that dates back to pre-Revolutionary days. Your Aunt Vicky liked it, knew I wanted land, and this old house was on the grounds. It wasn't all that much when I tackled it, but I think it's a gasser now, all the work I did on it; I nearly killed myself. How do you like my kitchen, Margo?"

It was a room about eighteen by twenty feet, warm, sunlit, with a restaurant-sized fridge, a separate freezer, a butcher's-block table. The drapes at the window were a Williamsburg print, cheerful and spanking clean.

It was a room a woman would like to be let loose in, make omelets and fondues, broil fryers and steaks, whip up custards and pies. "I just love it," she said.

"That's good enough for me. How about a drink before lunch?"

"Wonderful …"

He got busy with ice and vermouth. "You live here all alone?" she asked him.

"I do. A D.H. Lawrence character." He sent her a challenging look. "The town rake."

"Oh. Why not?"

"Nearing thirty and never married. You can imagine my reputation."

"I'll ask around," she said. "And if it's too infamous, I won't see you again."

He laughed, looking over at her.

"You're really a darling. Okay, sip a bit of this and tell me if I've done okay."

She sipped. "Absolutely perfect," she said.

He looked down at her, put the drink pitcher down on a table, and slung an arm across her shoulders. With a hand he stroked her chin, expertly, softly, affectingly. She stood there and liked it, and with his other hand he placed her head on his shoulder. "You fit nicely," he said, and now there was a different quality to his voice. A little rough, a little breathless.

"I like your style," he said. "I like your kind of woman. I'm not sure why I use the word, but I like your gallantry."

"That's a pretty corny speech," she said.

"I guess it is. What did I mean by it?"

"It was corny but appreciated," she admitted, and they sat down opposite each other at the butcher's-block table. "So much for badinage," he said. "What are you going to do about the house, Margo?"

"I've no idea at all."

"It's yours."

"Yes, I know."

"So?"

"What would you do?"

"Me? I'd say no, naturally. I wouldn't leave this farm, risky as it is—because farming is risky, anyone will tell you that—for Blenheim Palace."

"I wish I had something as affirmative."

They had a second drink and then wandered about the farm once more. They lay, stretched out, on a grassy little hummock, watching the clouds. "That's a dromedary," Doug said.

"That's a ballet dancer. See the long legs?"

"See the one over there…just beyond the big elm? It looks like my brother's profile."

There was indeed a face in the clouds, the outline of a strong brow and high-bridged nose. She laughed. "Your profile too," she reminded him.

"No, we don't look alike at all."

"You're twins."

"But we look different, are different."

"In what way?"

"He's a sterling character. I'm an odd lot. How is John, by the way?"

"What do you mean, how is John?"

"I don't see much of him."

"Why not?"

"My hours are different from his. I dropped in on Aunt Vicky during the day, mostly, whenever I could get away. He's a nine to fiver. Our paths seldom cross."

"You were together at the funeral."

At the word "funeral" she cringed, thinking about it All the townspeople, the minister, tradesmen, all there, in the church on Roxbury Road, with the ivy climbing over red brick walls, and the organ, thunderous. *We shall meet on that beautiful shore*…A sunny day, with flies buzzing in the summer somnolence.

The overpowering scent of flowers, massed on the casket, and on that little silken pillow Aunt Vicky's marble face, her strong, white hair arranged just so…rouge on her cheeks …

"Don't cry," Douglas said, and then, "All right, cry, maybe it's better you do."

It wasn't much of a cry, but she did shed tears and felt better for it. "It's just that I don't want her to be dead," she said, sitting up. "I'm not accusing anyone, but they never did have much time for me, my mother and father, and she gave me so much when I needed it. I did need it when I was a kid, and she was such a marvelous person. I never thought of her as old, though I thought of my parents as old. You take so many things for granted, you're sure someone will always be there. I mean, I can't accept the fact that she isn't *here*."

Her voice sounded hoarse to her. "You see, that house…well, in a way it's hateful to me. There it stands, safe and sound, up there on that hill, as if it were mocking the rest of us. She died and we'll die and our children will die, but the house is still there. I think I hate that house, and I think I want nothing to do with it."

She got up. "Am I keeping you from your duties, shall I go home?" she asked.

"If I'm needed, they'll call me. Let's walk a while."

They did that, hand in hand, over the rough, coarse grass. Talking about other years. "Remember the time we nursed the sparrow with the broken wing?"

"And then it flew and left us."

"Remember the time we got bombed on Gilby's gin?"

"And I threw up all over the crazy-quilt Aunt Lietitia made …"

Doug, back in the sunny kitchen, fried eggs and crisp bacon, and they had another drink. "I've enjoyed today," Margo said. "Oh, so much. Thanks, Doug, thanks very much."

She drove off. Rounding the bend, going past the cross-bar fence, she looked back. He was standing there, a big, healthy man with an arm raised. She waved back. So there were men like that, men who tilled fields and loved their acres, men who lived in quiet, sun-filled farmhouses, and rose with the dawn.

•••

When she got home there were two callers. The Reverend John Paul Jones was there, in his clerical collar, from the First Methodist Church, and Mrs. Pride, an old friend of her aunt's. Pompey was serving them tea. The curate set his Haviland cup and saucer down on an end table and got up spryly, looking a bit like a great black crane on his pipe-stem legs.

"My dear," he said, and held both Margo's hands. "Needless to say—"

"How are you, Pastor? I haven't seen you for so many years. You still look exactly the same."

His eyes twinkled. "Not you though, my dear child. You were a skinny little tadpole when last I laid eyes on you. Look at you now! You remember Mrs. Pride, Margo?"

"Of course I do."

She gave the old woman her cheek, received a cackle in return to her greeting, and held a dry old claw in her hand. The veins stood out like ropes. "Sit down directly and have some tea," Mrs. Pride ordered. "Pompey makes it good and strong. Tend to her, Pomp, that will put hair on her chest."

There was laughter, in which the old woman joined. "Nice to see you, my dear, and looking so blooming. Thank the good Lord you're bearing up well. I won't offer you sympathy, never held with it. What happens happens, no use in crying over spilt milk."

The metaphor was apt; at the same time she uttered the words she made a great spill down the front of her drip-dry cotton dress, dabbed at it with a serviette and then shrugged it off. "Sloppy weather, my mother used to call me, but of course that was many many years ago. I do seem to be getting on, every day a new wrinkle; can't guess when I go to bed at night what I shall look like the next morning. One does lose one's vanity, though, and it's only when I look at old snapshots that I realize I was once pretty, like you, my dear. They said I was like Mary Pickford, she was a film actress, though I doubt you've ever heard of her. What are your legs like, my dear? I can't see the shape of them in those pants things."

"I'm sure they're as lovely as the rest of her," the minister said gallantly, and Pompey added, "Knock your eyes out, they would, that child has legs like a flapper. Here's your tea, Miss Margo, drink up."

"Thanks, Pomp."

Mrs. Pride hogged the conversation shamelessly, talking about the long ago, about George, her husband, dead now, and their two sons, one killed in "the Great War," the other (the baby) now head of a publishing firm in Cambridge, Massachusetts. "I always say to George, at least one of them lived. I'm quite comfortable financially, but it wearies me sometimes, the way he sits silently and looks at the television. Who knows whether he even hears me?"

Suddenly realizing her lapse, she screwed up her face. "Did I say George...I'm a bit mixed up...that is to say ..."

She rallied, cackled again and asked for more tea. Pompey poured it for her. "Got my memories too," he said. "Guess we all have, us old ones."

"And how is your dear wife, Pompey?"

"Dancing with the angels, I expect."

"I was once the best dancer in town. I had a mean ankle. I saw them all looking at it! Dear Reverend, have some more tea. And sit down, sit down! Take a load off your feet. I always did abominate a man who paced the floor."

"Just that I must run along now, my parishioners," he said hastily, and Margo went to the door with him. "For heaven's sake, don't ask her for dinner," he whispered in the hallway. "You'll have her for à week. She's senile, of course, quite harmless, but do send her home soon."

"I'm sure Pompey will be master of the situation," she said, smiling. "You'll come again, I hope."

"Yes, of course." He fished in a pocket of his coat. "I have something for you. It's a copy of the Service. I thought you might like to have it."

"It's so kind of you. I do appreciate it," she said, and he went off, down the long walk, on his heron-like legs, getting into his nice, neat Buick and waving as he drove away. She put the mimeographed sheet on the hall table, her eyes catching a word here and there…"Whosever believeth in me…I am the Resurrection and the Life…in my Father's house are many mansions …"

What had the organ played, in her absence? And had there been tears? Whose tears? She went back to the living room and the sound of Mrs. Pride's gabble and cackle. "You want some more tea?" Pompey was asking, long-suffering.

"Good heavens, I'm filled to the brim with tea. As a matter of fact, I find myself beginning to have quite an appetite."

"Guess you want to get home to make your dinner," Pompey said kindly, but with a firm glint in his eye. "You just run along whenever you've a mind to, Mrs. Pride."

The vaguely hopeful look faded from watery eyes. It had been a good try. In order to underline the fact that there was to be no forthcoming invitation to an evening meal, Pompey added, "And Miss Margo, if you intend to be ready for that *engagement* you got tonight, better be thinking of your shower and getting dressed."

"Oh, you have an engagement?" Mrs. Pride asked, vanquished at last. "Well, then, don't let me keep you. I must cook my asparagus anyhow."

"No real rush," Margo said, bleeding for age and loneliness.

"Well, then, just a few minutes more. It's such a pleasure to see you after all these years."

"But not for long," Pompey said, fixing Margo with a stern eye. "You got to get ready and you know it."

"Yes, Pomp." She poured out more tea from the ornate Georgian service and they sipped.

"Funny she never married, isn't it?" Mrs. Pride remarked. "She always did love children so. I never particularly cared about them myself, though I raised two sterling sons. However, ours is not to reason why. And now my dear, congratulations. Many congratulations, heartfelt congratulations."

"Oh?"

"You deserve it too, you're a most remarkable young woman, amiable is what I mean, beauty is skin-deep, but you've got more than that. A good, *decent* face, and a kind heart. I'm leaving Margo a fortune, she said, and I asked her, well, will she *appreciate* it? Now I've no doubts. You've been kind to me this afternoon, you got rid of that *tiresome* old man, that blackbird with the turned-around collar. I know his heart's in the right place, but he's so damned, deadly dull, and now we can have a good chat."

"Well, I—" Margo started to say, but was interrupted by a regally lifted hand. "I know you'll never misuse what she left you," Mrs. Pride said. "You'll put the money to good use. I can't see you spending it on frivolous things; any fool could see you have more intelligence than that."

"As a matter of fact," Margo said gently, "there's no money, Mrs. Pride."

"Yes, there is, there's a great deal of it, she told me so. Didn't they inform you, my dear?"

"My aunt left me this house, that's what you mean, isn't it?"

"I know she left you the house! She always said she would. Of course! I'm talking about the money."

"I guess she did have a great deal of money at one time, Mrs. Pride. But the years depleted it. She lived well, but she lived for a long time. There's no money now."

"Oh yes there is," Mrs. Pride said positively. "Now, I'm not saying that the others know about it. But there is, and I may have my crazy moments, but she and I were friends for many, many years. There's a fortune, and she told me so. Ask Mr. Bach."

"I did."

"And?"

"He said she died almost penniless."

The cackle came again, and the old eyes gleamed with excitement. "Tell it to the Marines," Mrs. Pride said. "So the old goat wasn't in on it! Now, I just wonder what she did with all that money? How much did she say? Yes, I remember. Fifty thousand dollars, yes, and she said with time it would be even more, that it was an investment and could only appreciate with the years. You mark my words, Margo, there's money here somewhere, and it belongs to you."

"Well, perhaps. And now, Mrs. Pride, I suppose I must start getting ready for my…for my evening."

"Oh yes, yes indeed. Well, the tea was very good, you tell Pompey I said so. And you won't forget what I said, don't listen to that rickety old Jim Bach, he's got some age on him and he never did know his knee from his elbow anyway. There's a fortune somewhere here, somewhere in this house."

"Where, under the floorboards?" Margo asked, smiling.

"Oh, I don't think she'd do a thing like that," Mrs. Pride said. "It's in a reticule, or some simple place like that. I daresay she didn't want the others to get their hands on it."

"The others?"

"The lawyer, the boys, everyone. It belonged to you and you'll find it, never fear. You're still in a hurry, are you?"

"Well, rather. We'll get together soon again."

"Tomorrow?"

Pompey popped out of the kitchen and came down the long hall. "Bye bye, Mrs. Pride," he said, opening the door for her. "Thanks for dropping in. Mind you be careful on the way home."

"I certainly shall. The roads were slippery with ice on the way over. I drove at a snail's pace."

She looked out and raised astonished eyes. "Why, no, it's summer, isn't it?" she said. "Oh, I am so glad about *that*, I do so dislike winter. Well, then, thanks for the tea."

She took Margo's hand and gripped it. "A lovely afternoon," she said. "Very lovely. Don't tell the others what I said," she added, with a conspiratorial look, and waved to Pompey. Then she trotted down the front steps and got into her ancient electric, its speed limit twenty or thirty miles an hour, and tooled down the driveway.

Oh, dear Mrs. Pride!

In her room, resting, she heard doors opening and closing, finally got up and showered, then changed. When she went downstairs Norma was there, arranging flowers in bowls.

"Oh, you're here, how nice," Margo said gratefully. "And the flowers look beautiful, Norma."

"You think so? Come on, let's do the dining room."

She gathered up an armload of blooms from a newspaper spread on the floor, and in the other room fell to work, arranging, rearranging, and then standing back. "You think just a touch more of the fern?"

"To me it looks perfect."

"You may be right. Too much of a muchness is…too much of a muchness." She laughed, and held out her hands. "I'll want to wash," she said.

"Use my bathroom."

"May I? And will you keep me company?"

"Yes, certainly."

In the bathroom off Margo's room they chatted while Norma soaped her hands, applied perfume to her neck and forehead, and did a few things to her face. "Too much color?" she asked.

"No, not at all. You have such wonderful skin."

"You should see me in the morning. There, I guess that will do it." She stood back and stared, then packed up her make-up kit. "Drinks won't be amiss," she said. "I had quite a day."

"Did you, Norma?"

"Yes. I was born lazy and yet I work harder than anyone I know. Isn't life odd? Oh, I *do* have too much color on!"

"No, it's really just right, Norma."

"Would your Switzerland school approve it?"

"That was, alas, long ago."

"Everything was long ago. What's for dinner tonight?"

"I don't know, it's nice to be surprised."

"It seems to me I smell roast lamb."

"I hope so, I'm fond of lamb."

"Me too. Let's go, shall we?"

"After you, my dear Alphonse."

It was roast lamb, with a delicious, crusty outside. The potatoes were *au gratin*, there were buttermilk biscuits, and for dessert rhubarb pie.

"What did I do today?" Margo said, when asked. "For one thing, I visited Douglas at the farm."

"Did you now," Norma said, smiling, but John was silent on the subject.

"He seems to be doing quite well," Margo said. "Don't you think so, John?"

"So far," he agreed.

"Don't you approve of his venture?"

"It isn't *that*," he said. "It's just...a drought, a wet season, a cyclone, if you will, could wipe him out. Insurance doesn't cover an act of God."

"I think Doug's terrific," Norma said. "And so do you. I can see that, Margo. And then what did you do?"

"Came home and found the minister here, and Mrs. Pride, who gave me the electrifying news. It seems I've been left a fortune."

"Really?" John said, smiling.

"Her exact words."

"Did she say where it was?"

"No."

"Poor old soul," Norma said. "If you come across it, buy me a steak dinner with champagne and caviar?"

"It's a promise."

"Well, until that there fortune shows up, I'll make the most of being here for such time as God sees fit. Time's almost up for old Pomp. Today Brand Manor, tomorrow Missus Alberson's rooming house."

"*Sic transit gloria mundi,*" John murmured.

"I don't know what that means, but it would sound dirty coming from anyone but you, Mr. John."

"Pompey, *darling*," Margo said, smiling, and Norma laughed.

"There's only one Pompey," she said. "And I love every inch of him."

"The feeling's mutual, Miss Norma."

Later, they played canasta on a card table. Margo kept looking at John, wondering why his face was so different from his brother's. It was the expression, she decided. Sober John, laughing Douglas. They finished the game, had brandy and some idle conversation;

then Norma drove home, and the house became quiet. John locked up; Margo went upstairs and roved restlessly in her room. This was her home, her only home. And, by a quirk of fate, it now belonged to her. She gazed at herself in a mirror, without really seeing the face reflected there, and then prepared for bed, where the white curtains, lifted by a soft breeze, billowed inwards. A bullfrog croaked, tree toads sang. She slept and then woke, thinking she was in the Provence, in France, with the cicadas singing. *No, I'm here*, she told herself, and slept again, an arm flung out over the coverlet.

•••

It came so suddenly that she jerked in her bed. Her head raised from the pillow. *What was that?*

And knew instantly.

It was the telephone.

Darkness outside, only the faint light of a half moon. Darkness…she looked at her bedside clock. It was a few minutes to one, and the telephone was ringing on the landing.

No, she thought, stiffening. *Don't let it be that again.*

The bell shrilled, insistent. *I won't answer*, she told herself, pulling the sheet over her head. *I won't, I won't.*

It stopped after a while, and she pushed back the sheet. Lay, wide awake now, waiting. Five minutes later it rang again. Pealing outside in the thick dark, angering her, frightening her. "Please," she said aloud. "Please don't do this …"

It stopped.

But it will ring again, she thought. She knew it, of course. Of course she knew it. And stifled a scream as it rang again. Ring… ring…ring …

She sprang up and dashed outside, picked up the receiver. "Hello," she said. "Hello. Who is this? Who is this calling me at this hour?"

Silence, but not quite silence. That faint, eerie breathing. Almost not there but *there*…a suspiration…it was like some ghastly nightmare. There was a person who chose to ring her up in the wee hours of the morning, and not say anything, simply let his presence be known. He was there, he was breathing, he was alive and horrible and —

"What do you want?" she shouted. "What do you want? If you do this again I'll have you tracked down, don't think I can't! I'll move heaven and earth …"

She broke off and listened. There it was, the sinister, quiet sound of someone breathing …

She banged the phone down. Walked up and down the hall. *Don't let it happen again*, she prayed, walking up and down, back and forth. *It's enough now, don't let it happen again.*

The phone rang.

Now I will truly go mad, she thought, and ran to the instrument, looking at it, cursing it, wanting to tear it out of the wall. It rang, rang. Maddened, she plucked the sampler off the wall, GOD BLESS OUR HOME, held it in her hands and then dashed it against the door frame. The glass splintered and flew, the frame twisted and warped in her hands.

The ringing stopped.

What have I done, she thought, and groped her way, careful of the scattered glass, to a lamp. Her room sprang into view, cozy, hospitable. She pulled some tissues out of a box in the bathroom and went out into the hall again. Painstakingly, she swiped at the floor, wiped up the splinters of glass, then picked up the sampler and laid it on top of the lowboy. It was undamaged, only the glass had shattered.

The phone rang again.

This time she grit her teeth, marched out to the corridor, took the receiver off the hook. *There*, she thought. *There. Now try to terrify me. You can ring until hell freezes over, and I won't hear it.*

Then she stalked back to her bedroom, closing the door.

In the bathroom she filled the basin and plunged her face into it. Cold, cold, good country water.

She dried her face and stood thinking. Pondering. Because it was crystal clear to her—any thinking person would have gotten the message—that someone was trying to frighten her. She didn't know who, or why, but that ringing in the hours between dark and dawn was to scare her, to make her want to go away, to drive her from her own heritage, the house the townspeople called Brand Manor.

She left a lamp burning when she got into bed again. It attracted insects, gnats, small night moths and little flying things with gauzy green wings. She didn't care a bit. Better the tiny pests than dark and somber dreams.

She simply couldn't bear to lie, tense and spastic, in the dark. *It's been a long time*, she thought, *since I had to have a night light, to protect me from nameless terrors.*

Grimly, she admitted it.

Grownups had nightmares too.

CHAPTER SIX

Pompey had to wake her; she was dead to the world. She seemed to hear his knocking from a great distance. "It's me, Miss Margo," he said. "You awake? Wake up."

She rolled over on her back. "Come in," she said, and her voice sounded thick.

He walked in, saw her fatigued face and clucked. "You been crying," he murmured. "But that don't do no good, darling."

"It was the telephone again," she said, sitting up. "And it really got to me. Never mind, I can't afford to flake off. Something's going on, and I've got to be ready for it."

"The telephone again?" he said, sitting down on the bed. "Again?"

"Didn't John hear it?"

"No, or he would have said something. Me, I didn't either. Now we got to do something about this."

"Like what?"

"Get the law on them."

"On who?"

"Even here there's changes," he said. "Crazy young kids; you don't know what they're up to."

"Do you mean hopheads? But what would they have against *me?*"

"They read the papers, about you inheriting this house. Maybe they're having some fun. I can't think of nothing else."

"I don't know, I don't know. In the light of day it doesn't seem so fearful. But I just dread night coming."

"We'll talk about it some more. Right now you come down for your breakfast. Griddle cakes, maple syrup. Little sausages. Come on; you can brush your teeth later."

At the head of the stairs she reminded him of how he used to slide down the banister. "I remember," he said. "You was a tomboy, Miss Margo."

"It was because of the boys. Everything they did I wanted to do too, and then some."

"Which reminds me. Mr. Douglas sent over two nice little pullets for dinner. Sent over a recipe too, something fancy, some French name to it. Come on, I'll show you."

"Was he here?"

"No, not him. Lucas, one of those who fields for him, stopped over on the way to the farm."

She sat at the table, eating her wheatcakes and studying the recipe. It was for *Coq au Vin*, clipped from an item by Craig Claiborne, from an old issue of the *New York Times*.

So he isn't just a farmer, she thought, for some reason pleased. *He must have the paper sent to him from the city.* She read the recipe aloud to Pompey.

Take one pullet, three to four pounds, salt, dry well, flour and brown on all sides. Season, add herbs (tarragon, thyme, paprika and bay leaves). Add one and a half cups of chicken broth and red wine (claret or burgundy). Cook for thirty minutes, add small white onions and cooked fresh mushrooms (about half a pound). Garnish with parsley.

"You mean to say he sent the pullets and this recipe too?" she asked.

"Yes, honey, and some beefsteak tomatoes and nice brown eggs. We got a larder-full."

"Wasn't that nice of him."

He grinned at her. "Don't think he did it on account of me," he said. "Looks like he got a weak spot for someone else. Not mentioning no names."

She grinned back. "Simply platonic," she said, and when she finished her breakfast went right to the phone. "Hello," the pleasant voice said.

"Hello, Santa Claus."

"Oh, it's you," he said, and his voice deepened.

"Thanks for the largesse," she said. "We'll dine royally tonight."

"Nothing at all. I sent it over because I had originally planned for you to be here for dinner this evening, only my cow's dropping fast. What do you think about all this animal husbandry?"

"I think it's terrific. I hope you'll send me a birth announcement. What's the baby's name going to be?"

"I was thinking of Margo…that is, if it's a girl."

"Feel free, I'd be honored. I'll be her godmother. I don't suppose we could have her christened in church, could we?"

"I'll call up the minister right away."

"I'll have to wear something very special for the occasion."

He laughed. "Okay, honey, enjoy your dinner."

When she hung up she went back to the kitchen. "I just called Douglas to say thank you."

"Did you, now?"

"Because it was so nice of him."

"Things happen fast around here."

"Nothing's happening."

"No, of course not," he said. "No better man ever made than that Douglas. John too, both of them. You think about it twice. Your aunt always said, 'That child belongs up here, only she don't know it yet.' Now what you going to do today?"

"Enjoy being here. I'll take some pictures; I'm a photographer."

"That's my girl."

Ed Corliss was in the living room when she went down the hall, quietly working away, his face serious and intent. She hadn't heard him come in; he had keys, of course. She said, "Good morning, Ed," and he looked up quickly.

"Oh, good morning, it's a fine day, isn't it?"

"Too nice to be indoors," she said, and going up to her room, selected two cameras—one long lens, one for close shots—then went down again and started her work. The back of the house, in particular, interested her. It was diametrically in opposition to the front, which was in the traditional Georgian style, with its dormer windows, gambrel roof and Mount Vernon veranda. It was what one saw from the road: just that cold, perfect facade, in the best Colonial manner, and the beautiful doorway with its fanlight.

But from the back the house had a different aspect. For one thing, there was the "stoop," a long, rustic veranda running the width of the house—quite unusual in a mansion of this type—and above it, off the second-floor bedrooms, an iron balcony, like that of a residence in Louisiana, with curlicues and gingerbread, and a riot of color from the plants in heavy iron urns that studded its length.

It was, of course, an afterthought, and might have detracted from the famous house. Yet many architectural buffs had praised the later adjuncts. For example, one renowned critic had written: "The trimming at the back of the Brand House may seem to some a bastardization, but to these eyes it only serves to set this manor over and above others of the period. To my mind, these florid embellishments have charm and livability, and do nothing to despoil the chaste front of the historied house. Rather, they seem a delightful surprise and astonishment. To sit just outside one of the upper bedrooms, on that long, wide balcony, is a delight. Furthermore, the southern-plantation stoop, so out of place in an upstate New York manor house, is pure whimsy, and takes nothing away from the house's value ..."

The hours sped by as Margo, taking snapshots, lay now on her stomach, then on her back. It was a happy, rewarding morning, and when at noon Pompey came out and called, "Lunch!" she could scarcely believe the time.

It was lamb chops and tomato slices and iced tea, with cottage pudding for dessert. Ed Corliss lunched with them, and the three of them spent a pleasant hour in the sun-filled dining room. Where had he studied? Margo asked; he said Williams College, then had come home and taken a job with Mr. Bach. Was he married? No.

"Going steady, Ed?"

"More or less," he told her, but didn't elaborate.

He was a very *quiet* young man, no fun at all, but he did give her a wonderful present. "Letters," he said, when they left the dining room. "I'm sure you'll enjoy reading them. The ink is very faded, but you can make out the gist of them. They're from the sea captain, Benjamin Brand, to his wife Lavinia."

"Where did you find them?"

"In the desk in the Long Room," he said, meaning the living room and using the name indigenous to its time. "I'm sure they're of great historic value, not in monetary terms, you understand, but for future generations."

She thanked Ed and took them up to her room, where she settled down to read them, stroking the wrinkled, parchment-thin paper, yellowed with time. And as Ed said, the ink was so faded in spots that some words were almost illegible. Love letters didn't differ much from century to century, Margo thought…the same phrases, the same sentiments, the same aching longing transmitted from those parted by time and circumstance. A young wife had once waited eagerly for these missives and, upon receiving them, had curled up, perhaps in front of a roaring fire, and with beating heart read them, read them again, and yet again.

Then laid them aside, to be picked up next day and the next, and so many times that the paper had gone limp, had shriveled, and was now little more than dust. *And that woman and that man begat other women and other men who begat me*, she thought. And now here she was, catching yet another glimpse of her forebears, those who came ahead of her and just as surely as God made little green apples had brought her into being.

The first letter was dated July 29, 1847.

"Dear Lavinia:

"We rounded the Horn this morning, a bright, clear day, all men on board in good spirits. How are my wife and my dear Children? I hug you all, and hope to be home for the year end Holidays. To catch you under the Mistletoe. I would kiss you so soundly that you might cry out for help. I can hear you saying, Papa, get me away from this great bear of a man.

"It has been a calm sea and a calm voyage, our cargoes duly deposited and monies paid. Dr. Tippe had two men on the operating Table, one for Tonsils, the other for Inflamed Appendix, both men recovering very well. Say hello to the Baby for me, keep the other Children safe and well too."

The second date was September, 1847.

"Dear Lavinia:

"The First Mate is down with scurvy. It bodes ill, but we hope to be in Safe Harbour soon. We lost time, due to a Typhoon, and one of our men died of Natural Causes and was buried at sea. I read the Service and had a stiff Tankard of Ale later, to dull my sensibilities. Embrace our Children for me, hold them dear. I long to be with you all."

The third letter bore the date November 18, 1847

"Dear Lavinia:

"Another burial at sea. Mr. Hodkins fell ill with a Fever of the Chest, gasped out his Dying Hours. There was nothing to be done. Draped in the Flag of our Country he was lowered over the side into the Great Waters.

"On a lighter note, my Darling. I am posting this in the Island of Mauritius, I knew in my heart that I would not be home for Christmas, due to Unforeseen Events, the usual Delays that accompany a long sea Voyage. But there was a Great Ball here, which was very Nice, given by Lady Gomm, the Wife of the Governor. It was Festive and Gay, although I would have given Much to have been, instead, with my Family.

"And now, due to my Rank and Prestige and because my men find me an amiable Captain, ten of my crew have sent Christmas letters, they should arrive at about the same time that this Letter arrives. Well, we got a bit heady on Rum, and it was decided that, in lieu of my Presence, there would be Missives for you, which I hope you will enjoy. They are really Fine Men, and when we touch Home Port you will, I am sure, turn your attentions to a fine Turkey Dinner for them, and so show our Appreciation."

All the letters were signed "Your dear Benjamin."

And then, like another windfall, the rather crude messages from the crew. Varying little, all substantially the same. Addressed to "Dear Madam," with brief felicitations and hopes for a Happy New Year to the captain's Wife and Family. The names were the names of the period: Noah, Ephraim, Jonathan, Justin, Ezekiel, Amos, Abraham, Moses, Ishmael, Luke. Ten of them, with their warming little messages, ten fine men who had sailed the seas before the age of steam saw the last of the Yankee Clippers.

How fantastic, how exciting, Margo thought, and for a wild moment she *was* Lavinia Brand, tearing open the letters, crying, laughing, showing them to her children, her dear children.

Years ago, *years* ago…a century and a quarter ago, and yet, worn though the letters were, faded though their ink might be, and the senders dead for lo, these many years, the people who had lived those lives and those years seemed as alive, if not more alive, than what was around her. *I love the past,* she thought passionately, and went down to thank Ed Corliss for the find.

"They are lovely letters," she said. "Thank you, oh, so much, Ed. I can't tell you."

"They belong to you," he said. "They're not real property."

"What do you mean by that?"

"I mean, not like the house, or the furnishings, or the paintings, you understand."

"But mustn't I have them registered?"

"If you like, but it doesn't matter. The letters are oddments, curiosities, if you like. Like the old family Bible, which happens, at the moment, to be in Mr. Bach's keeping. If I should come across, for example, a letter from George Washington or Robert E. Lee, or something of like significance to the country of which you are a citizen, then that finding would be of general significance and would, per se, have to be registered and there would be a consultation with the Smithsonian Institute in Washington."

"But these don't fall into that category?"

"No, they're just old family letters and I'm delighted they gave you pleasure."

"Pleasure? Why, they moved me to tears," she said. "And again, Ed, thanks very, very much."

"You're quite welcome," he said, rather awkwardly.

She went outdoors, lifting her face to the sky, the sky that Benjamin Brand had gazed on, and all the others who came after. In foreign ports that man of the sea had longed for the landscape of home, had attended balls and been, according to his own account, a "popular" Captain.

Then she spotted Norma's car. Norma often came over on her lunch hour to do the flowers. Surely she'd have time for coffee and a chat. She made her way round to the back. "Oh, there you are," she started to say, and then realized that Norma wasn't alone.

She had her arms filled with blooms. Her head was slightly bent as she looked down at someone on the grass. Her neck was long and slender, her posture infinitely graceful. She looked like the Primavera, the long, luxuriant hair falling over her shoulders, her high, perfect cheekbones with the rich, tanned skin stretched tight, like satin. *That's what I call a picture*, Margo thought, and as the girl turned at her call, Margo had a quick glimpse of dark, intent eyes, as if…as if…

As if she were under a spell. She stood there, for another moment, stock still, her eyes vague and distracted, and with that strange, odd look.

"It's only me," Margo said.

One more strange moment and then Norma responded. "What are you doing home on a beautiful day like this?"

"I've been taking pictures," Margo answered, and then someone stood up, rising from the grass. *I don't know you*, Margo thought. *Who are you?*

It wasn't just a man. It was a superman, with great, ox-like shoulders, bare to the waist, a chest like a bull, covered with strong, dark hair, and the muscles of his arms rippled as he lifted his hand in a kind of salute. He stood well over six feet four, had a dark, handsome face, reckless eyes, and a bravado of manner that was faintly unpleasant.

"So this is little Margo," he said.

"You remember Ben," Norma said. "Ben Blough? The *enfant terrible*, the one who used to steal our clothes when we went swimming?"

It came back now. A big, burly boy with tight black curls, a bully, yet with an indefinable allure.

"Margo, Margo, how's your cargo?" It had always sounded nasty, though she was sure he hadn't meant anything in particular by it. "Cargo" was the first word that came to his mind to rhyme with her name.

"Hello, Ben," she said. "Of course I remember you. You were rather tormenting."

"Was I?"

His eyes on her, insolent. "Yes," she said. "You were."

"I've changed," he told her. "I'm a good boy now."

"That's nice," she said mildly, and Norma said quickly, "I don't believe him either." After which she explained that Ben had done a good deal of the gardening about the place for several years.

"He's good with growing things," she said, and Ben bowed low. "Thanks a million," he murmured.

"Well, I must get these done," Norma said hastily, scooping up an armload of flowers. "I'm on my lunch hour."

"But what about your *lunch?*"

"Don't worry about that; I'll order a sandwich from the drugstore later. Get back to work, Ben."

He said, "See you again, Margo."

"Yes, of course."

"Don't mind him," Norma said, as they gained the house. "Some people never change, never better themselves."

"What does he do besides some gardening here?"

"Odd jobs. Never went beyond the eight grade. All brawn and no brain. Now I must rush."

Margo followed as Norma made centerpieces and charming little set pieces for end tables. "I should do the upstairs, but I haven't the time," Norma said. "I'll tend to it this evening."

"You love this house, don't you?"

"Oh yes. It's a big part of me."

"We all love it," Margo said. "It doesn't belong to me, it belongs to all of us."

"Silly girl, it belongs to you. Forgive me, I must run along."

"You'll come to dinner tonight?"

"If you like."

"I want you to."

"Then I'll come." She dropped a quick kiss on Margo's cheek and rushed out, dashing off in her car, raising pebbles. Later, Margo went out to the back of the house and looked out again. Ben was still there, busily attacking his job, sweating profusely. He was using a spade, digging into the ground, his powerful biceps quivering with his exertions. "How often does he come here?" she asked Pompey.

"Him? Oh, about twice a week, maybe three times a week. A good worker, that Ben. Soon I call him inside, give him a cold beer."

"What do you think of him?"

He looked up, astonished. "Think of Ben?"

"Yes."

"Fine boy. Not much gray matter, but he gets along. Couldn't hold an office job, but that's nothing against him, neither could I."

Well, after all, live and let live, she thought, collecting her cameras again. Ben looked up when she came out. She nodded and smiled, and went about her business. He went about his, too. Yet as she positioned herself for the best shots, she felt his eyes boring into her back, felt that he was watching her. Half an hour later Pompey came outside. "Ben, how about some cold beer?"

"Great," Ben said. "Be right there."

"Miss Margo, the sun's beating down on your head. Don't get no sun-stroke. Iced tea, maybe?"

"No, I don't want anything, Pompey."

Ben, as he started toward the house, went a little out of his way to pass her. She was steadying a tripod. Startled, she felt his warm breath on her neck, turned abruptly.

"Don't get a sun-stroke," he said.

"I'll manage," she said, evenly.

"Sure you don't need any help, Miss Margo?"

He put a hand on her arm. It flamed through her. She drew back, shaking herself free. "No help needed," she said coolly, and he flashed a brilliant smile, white teeth gleaming in his darkly-tanned face, and then he went over the velvety grassland into the house.

Her arm still burned from his touch. Talk about animal magnetism…she remembered Norma standing there, looking down at him, rapt and tense …

She felt it. Norma felt it too.

She didn't wait for Ben to finish his beer. She gathered up her gear and took it inside and up to her room. *That's enough for today,* she thought, but it was only because of Ben Blough. There was something eerie about him, something unpleasant. *This man is dangerous ...*

Was that Julius Caesar? she asked herself, going up the stairs. *Or Hamlet?*

Anyway, Shakespeare.

CHAPTER SEVEN

She was downstairs, waiting, lonely for them all. John came first, clothes sticking to his skin. "What a rotten day, the heat and all that," he said, and ran upstairs for his shower.

Then Norma arrived, sniffing. "What's that I smell that makes my mouth water?"

"Doug sent over a feast from his farm; wait and see."

"He did?"

"It was nice of him, wasn't it?"

"Men are nice for a reason. Do we have a budding romance in our midst?"

"He's too concerned with his livestock. Now don't be silly, Norma."

"Oh, I see. I grant you he's good to look at."

"Possibly."

John came down, dressed in spanking white linen pants and a navy blazer with gold nautical buttons. "What's the occasion?" Norma demanded.

"What do you mean?"

"All dolled up like that."

His smile was forced.

"Or are we expecting Princess Grace?"

He ignored the taunt with a pleasant smile and went to the liquor cart. "You see, they fall like flies," Norma said, winking at Margo. "First Douglas, now John."

"Only a long and valued friendship keeps me from giving you a slap in the face," John said, bringing over their drinks. "How are they?"

"Perfect," Norma said, taking a sip. "But then, everything you do, John, is—"

"Perfect," he said imperturbably.

They've had a fight, Margo thought. Anyone *can* see that. Why?

"What did you do today, Margo?" John asked.

"Took pictures of the place. When they've been developed, I'll show you the results."

"How nice," he said, politely, and the doorbell rang. He looked up, his eyebrows raised. "Who do you suppose?" he asked.

"The Minister," Norma hazarded. "With a jar of calves' foot jelly."

But it was Douglas. His voice was unmistakable. He walked into the Long Room, asking if there was any chance of sponging a meal. "Another *man*," Norma cried, and sprang to the martini pitcher. Doug sat down, reaching out for the drink that was offered to him.

"Pretty good," he said. "Who made this, Margo or Norma? Whichever one, I offer my hand in marriage."

"I made them," John said.

"Hell, how was I to know that?"

Norma's laughter pealed out; Pompey heard the jubilation and looked in. "Why, Mr. Doug, you came to eat up your nice little pullets?"

"I came to see beautiful women."

"You came to the right place." He went off, chuckling.

"He's right," Doug said. "Nevertheless, I remember two skinny, scrawny kids…screeching when you got a splinter in your foot."

"You and John weren't exactly young Greek gods either," Norma retorted. "You both looked like bums and smelled worse, with those stinking, unwashed jeans."

"Besides, you were patronizing," Margo pointed out.

"Shall we let them get away with this, John?"

"Not on your life. We'll send them to bed without supper and a spanking to boot."

They sat there in the living room, badgering each other as of old, oblivious of the wide arch at the head of the room where generations of Brands had been married, and the camel-backed sofa and the tea-caddy lamps and the porcelains brought from the East on long sea voyages, and the Aubusson carpet mended many, many times, and the Coromandel screen. Aunt Victoria had said: *"You see that chair, Margo? Do you know who sat in that chair?"*

"Who?"

"A man named Marie Joseph Paul Ives Roch Gilbert du Motier. He was a French Marquis."

Aunt Vicky, relenting, seeing the uncomprehending eyes of a child. *"All right, he was called La Fayette. Does that ring a bell?"*

La Fayette…La Fayette…A hero to a romantic little girl.

"He was wounded at Brandywine, he had a limp after that. In 1824 he made a triumphal tour of this country, where he was greatly revered, and he sat in this house, in that chair, a guest of the Brand family."

Doug sat in that chair now. The tapestried covering had been done over who knew how many dozens of times, but it was the same chair the Marquis de La Fayette had sprawled in, his shining boots polished to a turn, his medals and decorations gleaming, one of the heroes of the American Revolution. She pictured Douglas in full army regalia, a glittering saber dangling from his lean hips, and suddenly the face of her childhood friend became the Marquis' face, with the high-arched nose, the firm, arrogant mouth, and the dark, inky eyes.

And Aunt Vicky saying, *"You must learn, darling, for one day all this will be yours."*

She sat up, startled. She heard the words as clearly as if they had been uttered at this moment…clear and firm, and her aunt's head nodding, encouraging, and then the hand weaving through her hair.

"You have hair like Iseult."

"Who was she?"

"You don't know about Iseult and Tristan and King Mark?"

"Not yet."

"Then let's sit down, and I'll read you Robinson Jeffers."

"Are you there?" Douglas asked, waving a hand in front of her face.

She came to with a start. "I'm sorry," she said. "I was just remembering."

His face sobered. "Okay," he said. "Okay." And shortly thereafter Pompey barged in and said dinner was ready, come while it was piping hot.

The *Coq au Vin* was succulent and tender, there were whipped potatoes with brown gravy, corn on the cob. "How's the chow?" Pompey asked.

"Indescribably delicious."

"Mr. Douglas deserves the thanks for it."

"Shoot," he said. "All I did was furnish the raw materials."

"And the recipe," Margo reminded him.

It was Douglas who suggested that they have coffee and brandy on the back stoop. "It's what we used to do years ago," he said.

"Oh, let's," Norma said. "It's still light enough."

It was about eight thirty when they settled themselves there, and the sky was streaked with pinks and purples. It was John who dusted off the redwood chairs, Douglas who carried out the tray of coffee and Courvoisier. They got comfortable, John sitting on the wooden steps and Douglas perched on the railing that ran the length of the rustic veranda, his back braced against a supporting pillar and his legs swung up to the neighboring post.

They toasted the house, each other, and drank another one for good luck. They chatted animatedly, four people who had known each other as children, and as adults had come together again. It was lovely, it was heartening, and yet, and yet …

There was a ghost present: *I feel like an interloper*, Margo thought. Beyond, in the gathering dusk, lay her aunt's gardens, day lilies and stock, pinks, hydrangeas blue and violet, marigolds the color of the sun, phlox, peonies, glory bushes. Aunt Vicky, outraged. "Japanese beetles! Margo, get the spray ..."

And Margo, with her small hands, manipulating the heavy can. "More force, child, we must save the blooms from enemy invaders; it's a war to the death."

And this too will pass away, she thought, watching the others. Everything passed away, everything. "I feel a mosquito," Norma said. "Let's go in, I can't see my hand in front of my face, anyway."

"And I must get home to my labors," Doug said. "Four in the morning's my rising time."

In the bright light of indoors they blinked at each other. "Come again, Doug," John said.

"Sure, will do."

He held Margo's hand. "You're getting a tan; you look very pretty."

"She always was," Norma said lightly. "In spite of what you said before. I remember how I used to feel. Because Margo was so pink and gold and white."

"Nonsense, I was a skinny kid and always too tall. I wanted to crawl into a hole."

"Well, we're grown up now," John said. "Sometimes I wish we could go back."

"I don't," Norma said. "I hated my childhood. I'm happy it's over." She rattled her car keys. "I must leave. Early to bed, early to rise. Coming, Doug?"

"Yes." He leaned against the door frame, raising a jaunty hand. "Good drinks, good dinner, good company. And now, with a hey nonny no, so long until the next time."

The front door closed. "That was nice," Margo said.

"It was indeed," he said.

"I missed her here."

"Yes."

"I mean—"

She looked up at him, wanting some response. But there was none. He simply said, "Go on up, Margo. I'll see to things."

She said, "All right, John," and left him walking through the lower rooms, his heavy tread echoing through the silent house. It was very quiet, Pompey long in bed after his day's work, and no sounds from outside until she went into her room. There, the night insects sang, and leaves shivered in the trees, and the thousands of blooms in Aunt Vicky's garden waited for the morning sun. She fell asleep dreaming about La Fayette sitting in the tapestried chair, his long, elegant legs encased in spotless boots, his head thrown back and smiling indolently. When he got up to leave he would walk to the door with a slight limp, for he had been wounded at Brandywine.

• • •

The telephone rang.

It's the telephone, she thought, and then, in the thick dark, quailed. No. Oh, no. Not again. Not again …

She lay and listened. Very urgent, that. Ring, ring. Ring, ring, ring. *Damn it*, she thought. *Damn it, God damn it.*

After a while it stopped.

But by now, of course, she was wide awake.

The room, because of the three-quarter moon, was almost as bright as day. *Now try and sleep*, she thought, her face crumpling. She would never get to sleep again, not this night. *Damn it and God damn it …*

The telephone rang again.

No, she thought. *I won't stand for this.*

She scrambled out of bed, raced outside to the hall. "Hello," she cried, speaking into the receiver. "Hello, speak. *Speak.* Damn you, *say* something!"

There was only the quiet breathing.

"Leave me alone," she cried hysterically. "Stop doing this! Leave me alone!"

There was only the quiet breathing.

She slammed down the receiver, stood there quivering and, reaching out, plucked the receiver off and left it lying on the table. *That's what I'll have to do*, she told herself, her thoughts garbled and incoherent. *Just every night leave it off the hook…. Christ, why?*

She went back to her room, sat thinking. And then she tried to stop thinking. Now is the time for all good men to come to the aid of their party …

She thought she heard the busy signal, that irritating clack clack, but her room was too far away. She knew it was there, though—buzz buzz—and it was nerve-wracking.

Someone please help me, she thought. *Won't someone please help me?*

•••

In the morning she told Pompey.

"What am I to do?"

He rolled his eyes. "Let me find that no good, I'll flay him alive," he promised. "Son of a bitch, excuse my language. I just want to destroy him, the rat, the bastard, excuse my French."

"Someone has it in for me and I don't know who." She gnawed at a fingernail. "I thought I'd tell Mr. Bach about it."

He was scornful. "Him? He don't think about nothing but his law business." He tossed his gray head. "Maybe it's him that calls you, maybe in his second childhood."

"Pompey, for heaven's sake …"

"Fairy-like, doesn't know which end is up. Never did cotton to him. Brain, maybe, but nowheres else. Wouldn't trust him no further than I could throw a cat."

"Pomp, poor old Mr. *Bach*," she said. "That harmless old man."

"Seems like everyone's harmless, but just the same, someone did the calling, right?"

"Yes, but—"

"Then everyone's supect, ain't that so? Him too."

"Just the same, he's the last on my list," she said.

"If it was like it used to be, we could find out easy," he said discontentedly. "Operator would know. But these days, everything's dial. No way of telling."

"Yes, progress has its penalties," she agreed.

"Let me think about it," he said, dishing up breakfast. "You forget about it and let me think about it. Miss Margo, you want to get away from this place today. How about the Fair?"

"The Fair?"

"Dutchess County Fair. You have a good time. Cotton candy and apples on the stick. Hot roast beef sandwiches, ice cream. Everyone and his brother. Not far away, too."

"That sounds very nice, Pomp."

"Pretty good show. You don't find *that* in the city. Now I got to get these dishes done, and then mow the lawns on this hot day. No rest for the weary."

But he twinkled, kissed her on the cheek, and she ran upstairs for her handbag and camera. When she went down again, Ed Corliss was there, with his clipboard, attache case and hesitant smile.

"Good morning, Miss Brand."

"Oh, hi."

"Headed for fun and games?"

"Yes, I'm going to the Fair."

"Fine, you'll enjoy it." He set his attache case down.

"More tickets on furniture?" she asked.

"That's about it."

"Doesn't it bore you, rather?"

"I don't think about it."

"How long will all this take?"

"Several weeks."

"My word."

"You may not be here at the end of it, but it's your property until you decide to do otherwise."

"You mean *unless* I decide," she said.

"Of course that's what I meant," he said smoothly, and it gave her an odd feeling. Because he had distinctly said 'until you decide.' Once again she thought, *He has no charisma, he's a dull young man, not to my taste at all.* Out loud, she said, "Don't work too hard, Ed."

Then she got into her car and saw him looking out a window. She waved, but he drew his head back. *Funny guy*, she thought, and then gave herself up to the pleasure that lay ahead of her. It was another gorgeous day with brilliant sunshine, the beginning of July.

She sang as she drove. "The sun-burned hand I used to hold …"

She didn't need a map; she knew the terrain as of old. She was in Ghent at just past midday, and the Fair was in full swing, the sounds of it echoing through the limpid air. She bought an apple on the stick right away and bit into it. Sticky, sweet, bringing back other years. She walked about, snapping pictures, listening to fragments of conversation, and passed the time of day with this one and that one. Then she bought a few things, such as aprons she had no use for but which had been hand made by the "natives."

At a shooting gallery she threw away two dollars in dimes before hitting her target. "This little lady …" the barker said, bellowing it. The prizes were tawdry and worthless, and she settled for a paperweight with a winter scene and snow sifting down. She stuffed it, along with the rest of the junk, into a shopping bag that had DUTCHESS COUNTY FAIR printed on it.

The prize didn't mean anything: it was the affirmation, like a good omen. *We're all superstitious*, she thought. And when she wandered into the livestock section she saw Douglas right away. He was among a clutch of countrymen who were dickering over some animals. On the block was a big bull with wicked red eyes and terrible horns, and Douglas was calling his bid.

Needs it to stud his calves, Margo thought, *all very earthy and primal.* She stood fairly near him, and then he saw her. "Hello, bright-eyes," he said, grabbing her elbow. "Stick around, this won't take long."

She started getting very excited as the bidding went up. It was evident that Doug meant to have that bull. "Six hundred," he called out.

"Six fifty," someone else said.

"Seven hundred."

There was a short silence, then, "Seven fifty."

"Eight," Douglas said, his jaw set.

This time there were no more bids.

The gavel came down. "Going…going…gone!"

There was a round of applause, and the bull was loaded into a truck, goaded up a ramp, and the gate closed. "A good job done," Doug said, and told the man behind the wheel to drive home slowly and carefully.

"Roger and out," the driver said, and drove off, the bull bellowing.

"Aren't you ever afraid?" Margo asked.

"Only of women."

"I'll bet."

"And now that that's done, how about a drink?"

They left the Fair grounds and went into a local bar. "Don't order a cocktail," he warned her. "Just straight whiskey, with a chaser."

"If you say so."

"I do. I called the house. I wanted you to come with me, but you'd already left. Pompey said you were headed this way. Needless to say I was delighted."

"Really? How about your pregnant cow?"

"Doing her post partum exercises…she dropped around three this morning."

"Fine, fine. Girl or boy?"

"Girl, name's Margo."

She laughed. "Really?"

"I thought we agreed on that."

"We did. I'm very set up. I must knit her some baby things."

"She'd appreciate that."

"Then I'll get started right away."

"Tomorrow will do. How about another drink?"

"I could manage."

They were served, and he asked her what was new and interesting. "Nothing much," she said. "Unless you call a visit from the Minister and Mrs. Pride interesting."

"Oh my, your life here's very exciting, isn't it?" But then he smiled. "I happen to have a soft spot for old Mrs. Pride. I always thought that, if she had a parrot, it would say some shocking things."

She laughed. "You may be right. For instance, she told me Pompey's tea would put hair on my chest."

"That's only for starters. I've heard her say things that would… well, that you wouldn't believe."

"She's rather far gone these days, I fear."

"You mean out of it. Yes, I know."

"For one thing, she instructed me that Aunt Vicky had left me a fortune."

"Ah so?"

"I thought, of course, she meant the house. No, she insisted. I'm an heiress. Something about fifty thousand dollars, maybe more."

"In a piggy bank?"

"I said, 'Under the floor boards?' And she scorned that, said Aunt Vicky wouldn't be so nonsensical. She's under the impression that there's money somewhere, holed up in that house. In a "reticule," or some similar place."

"A reticule! The old dear …"

"Yes, she is, rather, but Pompey sent her home without dinner. I could have cried."

"I see his point, in all truth. So you've been left a fortune."

"According to Mrs. Pride."

"I can't quite see Victoria Brand depositing money in a Swiss bank, can you?"

"No. Or hiding it in a reticule either. She was such a straightforward person. Mrs. Pride told me not to tell the others."

"Meaning?"

"You and John. Mr. Bach. She doesn't seem to dig Mr. Bach, she called him an old goat."

"Well, he is, rather."

"He's a kindly old gentleman."

"Kindly old gentlemen sometimes conceal wicked interiors."

"You think he stole my fortune from my aunt?"

"He could have."

"What do you mean?" she asked, scoffing.

"Lawyers have power of attorney. Most of them. Probably Jim Bach did too."

"And now he's gloating, like Silas Marner, over the fortune she left me?"

"Damn his eyes."

"You're rather a bit of fun," she said.

"I was hoping you'd think so."

"Oh, Douglas …"

"Where'd you get those eyes, and what color are they, anyway?"

"Do I have to listen to this malarkey?"

"It's up to you, my dear."

"I have you in my power, you know. You have no means of transportation back to the farm. I can leave you stranded, circling around in the arid desert, crying for water and seeing mirages. I could do that, you know."

"You'd never be so cruel."

"Don't bet on it."

"Have another drink."

"I've had quite enough. I'll drive you back now, I can't bear to think of you going mad in the wilderness, poor thing. I've too kind a heart."

'I'll nominate you for sainthood. But you won't drive me back, not yet. I'm going to take you sightseeing."

"Really? Where?"

"To a little undersized community where, would you believe it, two witches were burned, according to the quaint custom of the times, accused of poisoning the immortal souls of a couple of misbegotten girls who claimed themselves under the power of the Devil and pointed a finger at their schoolteachers, aged twenty and twenty-one, respectively. So there was an auto da fe in the public square. This was, you understand, in the century immediately before the one which precedes ours."

"Do you mind if we don't talk about it," she said, shivering.

"Not at all. What's left is peaceful enough. I discovered it only a couple of years ago. As a matter of fact it was John who told me about it; he's the scholar, you know. It's off the beaten track, and what I want to show you is a little churchyard that's nearly three hundred years old. I go there at times when my psyche isn't all it should be. How about it, or do you have more glamorous things to do?"

"Hardly. I'd love to see your little churchyard." He paid the bill and they got in the car again, heading north. "It's about sixteen miles away," Doug said. He drove because it was easier, he pointed out, than giving directions. "How about lighting me a cigarette?"

She lit two and handed him one. "Tastes like your mouth," he said, smiling sideways.

"How would you know?"

"My fertile imagination," he answered and, smiling back, leaned an arm on the window, exhaling smoke. "Shall I put the radio on?"

"Not for me."

"Not for me either. Talk is better."

They chatted idly, sometimes discussing the problems of the day, sometimes reminiscing. Doug called himself an Ethical Humanist; she liked the sound of it. "Perhaps I am too," she said, and he remarked that if it was so it was another thing they had in common.

"What other?" she asked.

"Our childhood, after all."

"Yes, of course, Douglas."

"And a natural attachment for each other."

"Do we have that too?"

He turned to her, gave her a long, serious look and said, "Yes, we do," and then attended to the road again. There was a kind of vibration, to which she kindled, and she glanced at his handsome, browned face, his intelligent, alert eyes, and thought, *Take it easy, just take it easy.*

Was she falling in love with him?

They branched off at a picayune little railroad crossing, and came to a small church almost hidden behind shrubbery and tall elms. "Here we are," Doug said, and parked the car. The quiet was intense, the only sounds those of nature: the rustling of trees, bird-songs, the tinkle of a cowbell. "Let's get out," Douglas said, and they padded over leafy ground. "We'll go in and light a candle for Aunt Vick first, and then I'll show you the old graves."

The door was heavy and nail-studded, creaking open rustily, and then they stood in the gloom of an almost lightless interior. There were six narrow windows, three on either side of the little church in the wildwood, long and slender as needles, darkened and grimy with age. A small rose window accented the farther end, its jewel tones subdued by dust and neglect.

Yet there was a hushed, hallowed sense of respose and sanctuary about the tiny chapel. Pilgrims had knelt here, thanking God for release from tyranny; in the high, carved lectern a man of God had once thundered a message founded on the Gospel, and a small band of parishioners, forging their way in the New World, had sipped the wine and taten the wafer on their tongues. The figure of Christ on the Cross, primitive and writhing, seemed to be saying in the solemn stillness, "This peace I give unto you…not as the world giveth, give I unto you …"

"This is nice, isn't it?" Douglas whispered, and led her forward to the rows of flickering candles. He fished in a pocket and drew forth some coins, which he dropped into a tin box, the sound reverberating in the stillness. Then he pulled out a taper for her. She lit it from one of the flickering candles. *For my aunt,* she thought, and Doug lit another. They stood and watched the new flames flaring and then went out again.

Into the afternoon beneficence, the birds twittering madly. "Come on, honey, let's take a gander at the gravestones, they're older than God."

Dating back to the beginning of the country, they dotted the hillside. Long before the Declaration of Independence, in 1776, men and women and children had been interred here, laid in the ground to the sighs and cries and sobs of mourners. Headstones half-sunk in the earth, moldering flowers, overgrown grass. *Here lies Fanny Hayes, born 1691, died 1749 …*

An angel, in marble, wings spread. *God rest her soul …*

They sat quietly on an iron bench, painted white, listening to the sounds of nature, bird calls and leaves rustling. Douglas said, "I come here when I'm down, you know, down. It says something to me. That my life is only the continuation of what went on long before me. These people are my friends, and hell, a lot of them are probably my relatives. We're an ingrown lot here."

He bent toward her. "Don't grieve," he continued. "She was one of them too, and she handed down to us her own bit of history. Listen, Margo, she lived a good life, let's hope ours will be as good."

They walked on again, back to the car, and got in. "I just thought you'd like to see that," Douglas said. "What we came from, why we're alive today." He put the car in gear and smiled, the smile that made her think of the boy's smile of long ago.

"Now can we go some place lively?" he asked. "Have a drink, maybe two or three drinks?"

"Yes, Douglas."

"Light me a cigarette, okay?"

"Okay," she said, and they drove on, companionable, chatting idly, sons and daughters of the American Revolution. *Here we are*, she thought, *in the twentieth century, with all that behind us.* Humble, she looked out the window at the glory of the New World, of which she was part and parcel, a child of pioneers.

CHAPTER EIGHT

When she got home there were guests. Several women sitting sedately, and a murmur of voices. Pompey was presiding, very proper and polite, passing out little cakes on a silver tray. "Oh, Pompey, they look so delicious," a voice said, and then Margo was spotted.

"Here you are," someone cried, and she who had been away for so long recognized faces, grown older, but still recognizable. Women in whose kitchens she had once been given ginger snaps and chocolate chip cookies, and whose sons and daughters she had played with.

It was like a scene in a play; they sat there with their tea cups in their hands, wiping their fingers on tiny little squares of cambric. There was Mrs. John Ericson, whose son Sven had almost white eyelashes (there was a sizable contingent of Scandinavians in Cranford), Mrs. Gilbert Smythe, whose husband had sung tenor in the Methodist Church. The Minister's wife was there too, as stout as he was lean, with feet that dangled just short of the floor.

Good and worthy women all, and they had brought offerings: currant jam, preserved peaches, home-made bread. Estimable women, welcoming her with open arms…but privately Margo would have preferred an insane chat with old Mrs. Pride. Respectability shone in their scrubbed faces, good will beamed from sympathetic eyes.

And curiosity.

Naturally.

What, for example, was she, Margo, going to do about the house? Or about anything, for that matter. After all, she was a foreigner, late of European climes. "All those years abroad," one of the women said, leaning forward. "How does it feel to be back?"

"And doesn't the house look lovely?" another of them asked. "Just the way it always was when she—"

"Shush now," a voice warned. "Margo doesn't want to—"

"And how are your dear parents, dear?"

"Do they know about your being left Brand House?"

"Won't you come to church this Sunday? Matthew would be so happy."

"There's a supper on the twenty-third. And a Cake Fair next Friday. Outdoors, unless it rains, but we're praying it won't."

They ate Pompey's cakes, patted their mouths with their napkins, and at five promptly got up, in concert, to go. "Please come again," Margo said. "Thank you so much for everything."

"You'll be all right?"

"Yes, of course."

She saw them to their cars, looking after them, watching them drive away. She was unaccountably melancholy. Those women, with their tidy lives, they meant well, but somehow they had been upsetting. She wasn't her Aunt Vicky, who had entertained countless gatherings such as the one this afternoon, letting the homely conversation go in one ear and out the other. She was only Margo, and somehow this afternoon, with the burgher's wives, had been upsetting. They were on their way home, to their tidy houses and tidy kitchens, with their men returning from offices. *"Hello, dear, how was your day?"*

"Well, the children—"

"Got something cold to drink? My tongue's cleaving to the roof of my mouth ... "

The sound of the lawn mower out back interrupted her reverie. As she rounded the side of the house she saw Ben Blough at the farther end of the lawn, using the hand machine for trimming around flower beds. He saw her and waved; otherwise she would have retreated.

"Hi, there," he called, and she walked over to him.

"Aren't you working rather late, Ben?"

"I work whenever I have the time," he said. "There's a lot to be done around this place. Maybe I won't be able to get here for another day or two, so I do as much as I can when I can."

He turned his back on her, smiling over his shoulder, and pushed the mower in the other direction. There was something almost hypnotic in the whirring of the machine, and the lithe movement of his panther body. She watched him; at the pear tree he turned, coming toward her again, gleaming sweat on his naked torso. *If I could paint, I'd paint him*, she thought, and suddenly heard his muttered curse.

"Goddamn bugger ..."

He knelt, and bent to pick something up from the grass.

"What is it?" she asked, thinking that the meshes had hit a stone.

"Stupid goddamned frog."

She saw the thin stream of blood, and the yellowish mucus, the writhing, dangling legs. It was a small frog, and Ben had gone over it with the mower.

Her stomach turned, she stifled a scream, darted forward with a hand on his arm. "Didn't you see it?" she flung at him.

"I was looking at you," he said insolently.

The half dead thing bled in his fingers, sending a trickle down his wrist. "It's all right, I'll finish it off," he said, and dropped it. Picking up a good-sized rock, he raised his arm, aimed, and smashed down on the writhing creature.

"That did it," he said.

She closed her eyes, dizzy, turned and walked away. In the distance, he snarled, "What was I supposed to do, leave it suffer?"

"It's all right," she said, over her shoulder. "You did the right thing."

And he had. But she would never forget that brawny arm raised, the thud of the rock hitting skin and sinew. "Dinner will be ready soon," Pompey said, as she walked into the kitchen; and then he had a good look at her face.

"What's the matter, girl?"

"Nothing."

"You don't kid me. What's the beef?"

"Ben ran over a frog. It's all right, he finished it off."

"Miss Margo, this is the country. Happens all the time. Things like that. Last week a little phoebe bird fell out of its nest. Something got at it, a cat, I suppose. Neck tore open. Nothing for me to do but put it out of its misery."

"Yes, I know," she said, and he sat her down and made her a cup of tea. It was good, strong tea, bracing enough, but she was thinking about victims, small, helpless creatures who had to be put out of their misery. Nature was so inexorable, she thought, and the little phoebe bird, waiting for an act of mercy …

But She hadn't seen the phoebe bird; she had seen the toad.

Had Ben seen it too…and deliberately ran the mower over it? *Why should I think something like that*, she asked herself, but remembered the hard, pitiless face, the low forehead, a modern version of a Cro-Magnon man. *He's cruel, I know he's cruel*, she thought, and then heard Norma's voice.

"It's me again. You don't mind, I hope?"

"Mind! Norma, hello, are you worn out, did you work hard today?"

"I work hard every day, that's what days are for, aren't they? To work hard? What did you do today, my pet?"

"I went to the Fair."

"How was it?"

"Lots of fun."

"Did you win anything, like one of those awful dolls?"

"No, a paperweight. And Douglas was there, bidding on livestock."

"As was only to be expected."

"He bought a bouncing bull."

"With wicked, red eyes?"

"Oh, *such* a baleful expression."

"I knew you went to the Fair, Pompey told me when I came over on my lunch hour. You could comment on my handiwork."

"Norma, the flowers look beautiful. All the women admired them."

"What women?"

"We had a kaffee klatsch. Ladies Aid, from the Church."

"No wonder you look so pale and wan."

"It was rather out of my sphere. However. Make yourself at home. I want to quickly bathe and change."

"Want your back scrubbed?"

"No, but you can start the drink pitcher."

"Righto. Go on up now, come down all beautiful and glowing. You do look rather white. Why?"

"It was the toad."

"The what?"

"Nothing, I've already forgotten it."

But she hadn't. That arm raised, the stone smashing the wounded creature to a pulp. Well, what else was there to do? Pompey: "Had to put it out of its misery."

She went up the stairs and opened the door to her room. Closed it and then smelled the fragrance. On top of the lowboy an exquisite arrangement of cornflowers, marguerites and asparagus fern. When she bent to it, sniffing, there was a scrawled note.

These are for you from me…Norma.

It was an antidote to ugliness and small, lonely suffering. *I won't think of the toad,* she told herself, and touched the flowers with a grateful hand. What a lovely thing to find…Undressing, she looked at it once again and then got into the tub, half dreaming. The smell of searing meat drifted up from below; her mouth watered. *I should marry Pompey,* she decided. *He's the best cook in the country.* Climbing out of the tub she wrapped herself in a huge Turkish towel and heard the words of the marriage ceremony. *"Pompey, will you take this woman in sickness and in health, for better or worse, until death do you part?"*

"I do," Pompey said, and she threw the towel across the rack, bathed her warm, flushed face, and got dressed. In better spirits, she joined the others in the living room.

"Get busy on this," Norma said, handing her a drink.

"Yum," Margo said, sipping. "I've just had a proposal of marriage from Pompey; it was in a kind of bathtub dream."

"Congrats, may I be a bridesmaid?"

"Yes, you're to wear a long yellow dress with daisies in your hair."

"I'll start looking for one tomorrow."

They laughed companionably. "I have my odd and sundry fantasies too," Norma confided. "Once I dreamed I was walking naked through Britton Woods with the Minister. He chucked me under the chin and started becoming *very* familiar. I slapped his face. 'How dare you?' I said, and then woke up. I saw him on the street next day, and almost whopped him one. Poor thing, he looked so astonished at my mean expression. Of all people, the Reverend, poor old soul."

"If you had the temerity to walk naked through Britton Woods," Margo said severely. "It served you right when he got fresh."

"I agree. Oh, I agree."

"Listen, thanks for the flowers, Norma. I can't tell you how lovely it was to find them there, and your dear note."

"Just one of my small pleasures," Norma said. "Well, here's our friend. Hello, John, drinks are ready, help yourself. Margo went to the Fair today."

"That's nice."

"It was like being a kid again."

"She won a paperweight."

"Well well."

"And after that she entertained the Ladies Aid at tea."

"Really?" He looked over at Margo, made a wry face. "So they're starting to drop in."

"Apparently."

He pushed his dark hair back. "If nothing else does, *that* will drive you away."

"Oh, it wasn't that bad," she started to say, and then caught her breath. What he had said…what he had said …

If nothing else does, that will drive you away …

"I suppose they brought little treats," he went on. "They really are the salt of the earth, but just the same preserve me from them." He raised an arm and again dashed back his hair. "That's the trouble with this house. You can't pretend you're not at home. There's always someone home. Pompey, or Ben in the garden, or Clara, cleaning. How did you manage?"

She could speak again now, though her lips were dry. "Quite well," she said. "It wasn't a long visit. They got up, by some apparently prearranged signal, all at once, and went chugging away in their cars. And they did bring treats, nice ones, thoughtful ones. Things they made themselves."

The lock of hair fell over his forehead again. He was sitting with one leg thrown over the arm of a Hepplewhite chair, a long, lean leg, and his skin was lightly tanned, not bronzed from the outdoors like Doug's, but summer-darkened. She thought suddenly, *He's handsomer than Doug and he knows it and no, they don't really look alike. It's the personality behind the face that gives it individuality, even though nature made them from the same genes.*

He couldn't *have meant anything by that sentence*, she told herself. It had been just a random thing to say. And a day or two ago it wouldn't have registered.

A day or two ago …

Before the telephone calls ...

Yet the very first evening she had been here he had said something else, something she hadn't forgotten. *"Just like old times ... "* She couldn't picture Douglas saying such an insensitive thing. *What makes him tick?* she wondered, watching him. *What makes John tick?*

"Dinner's ready," Pompey said, clapping his hands in the doorway. "Come in, you all. Before it cools. I worked my butt off. Bring your drinks in with you."

• • •

Later, in bed, Margo thought about it again. What John had said. The words, in fact, rang in her mind: *Drive you away...drive you away...drive you away ...*

"Tomorrow being tour day," he had announced at dinner, "I'll be home at two in the afternoon. Just close the door to your room, Margo. It won't be shown, so don't worry about straightening it up."

She turned, trying to sleep. Tomorrow was a tour day, and in spite of what John had said, she would leave her room in apple-pie order, so he could show it if he cared to.

So better get some sleep.

She was overtired, though, it had been a long day. The Fair, the fresh air and activity, the slight strain of entertaining the Ladies Aid women (too much a reminder of her aunt), the vivid recollection of Ben Blough raising his arm and then lowering it ...

"That did it ... "

And the telephone outside.

At any minute it might shrill out, and she would jerk in the bed, stiffen.

The hell with all that, she decided, and got up to take a sleeping capsule. She went out to the balcony, smoked the whole of a cigarette, ground it out in one of the iron urns, and went back to bed.

It won't work, she told herself, *this time it won't work*. But even as she was thus informing herself, it worked. The moonlight bathed her still body, one arm thrown over the edge of the bed, and the rustling in the trees fell on deaf ears.

CHAPTER NINE

The bus arrived at a quarter after two. "You want to put in a word or two?" John asked Margo, but she quickly declined. "You know the tour, you can't have forgotten it," he said, but she told him she would only be self conscious and spoil the whole thing.

"Well, then, some other tour day," he said, and they went outside to welcome the waiting guests, about thirty of them. *It gives one pause*, she thought, and there was a quiet pride in her, that the history of this house was part of her own. John, in navy suit with cornflower-blue shirt and gold cufflinks, was very much the *grand seigneur*, and looking very handsome. The younger girls in the group exchanged glances which could only mean, *Isn't he groovy?*

His voice, dark and deep and well-modulated, carried well, so that even those in the back were able to hear, and Margo was reminded of such day tours in foreign cities. *"Everyone can hear, I hope? This is the Piazza Navona, one of the most beautiful squares in R-r-r-ome ... "*

"And now you see, ladies and gentlemens, zee Tour Eiffel, erected for zee Paris Exposition of 1889, voila ... "

She stifled a smile and followed. John said, "In this room is the tester bed where John Quincy Adams slept. Note the Deerfield blinds at the windows. In 1794 the chimneys were rebuilt, the new roof raised on the house in 1799."

He pointed out highboys—"from the Phillips house in Boston"—the vertical sheathing and fine paneling in the lower hall, the lustre ware and Lowestoft in the dining room.

"These pewter plates on the mantel," he said, "have long histories. The one on the right was brought to Salem, Massachusetts, from

England, with the advance guard of the Phillips family in 1630. The other two were imported by Nathaniel Brand about 1750."

He led them out to the back veranda. "This was called the stoop. Just where Nathaniel Brand got the idea for this typical southern adjunct to a plantation house is a conundrum, for it is known that he never spent any time south of the Mason-Dixon line."

"He must have known Southern people," a tourist suggested.

"He must and did," John said, smiling. "It's, of course, the only explanation."

The tour took an hour and a half. When they had all gone off in the chartered bus, John asked Margo if he had performed creditably. She said yes, more than that, and congratulated him. "After all, I've heard it just about forever," he reminded her, and went back to his office. She stayed there, remembering what she had just heard and whom she had first heard it from, her Aunt Victoria. Sighing, she lit a cigarette on the back veranda and looked out over the green meadow past the gardens and dreamed.

Pompey came out and asked her what she wanted to drink. Iced coffee, Gatorade, maybe something stronger?

"Nothing now," she said, thanking him, and alone again, looked across the meadow and the gardens and the tall trees, to the spire of the little church in Plunkett, a hand-span away at the other side of Justice Creek. It was very peaceful and very quiet, and after a while she fell asleep.

• • •

She must have slept the afternoon away, because when she woke the sun was lower in the sky and, although the day was still brilliant, there was a faint violet tint to it, and she looked at her watch.

It was just after five.

Then she heard the voices.

Very low, indistinct, and to her right, in the gardens. A man's voice and a woman's voice. *Oh, it's late,* she thought. *They're already home, and I must bathe and change.* She got up, a little stiff, stuck her packet of cigarettes into a pocket, and walked across the stoop to the steps. Someone said, "Now, listen, you just take it easy. You don't want to—"

There was a low rumble in answer…John's voice? And then the woman again, Norma, of course. "I said, stop that, don't you realize that—"

For some reason, Margo was wary. She went down the steps that led to the garden path and peered ahead, past the house. There was a quick glimpse of a flowered dress, long and floating dark hair…Norma. And then someone else…someone who stood tall and strong and powerful against the evening sky, his bronzed torso gleaming in the heat of the slanting sun, strong arms reaching out …

That's not John, Margo thought. That's Ben.

It was Ben, all right, and his arms, the biceps rippling with power, easy power, pulled Norma against him, forcing her head upwards, a hand thrusting through her hair.

"You're hurting me," Norma protested, in a stifled voice.

And Margo stood stock still, clenching her hands. *I knew it,* she thought. *I knew it …*

His enormous hands, holding up the wriggling toad, blood trickling down his wrists …

The sounds of the struggle were muted, but horrifying. Norma freed a hand and raked it down Ben's face. "Let me go," she hissed. "Let me go, you animal …"

Margo ran down the steps. Over Norma's head her eyes and Ben's met. Hers were blazing, his blinking with surprise. He released the other girl, who staggered slightly, grabbed at his arm for support. Then she turned. Her face was flaming red, her eyes filmed. For a moment there was absolute silence.

Then Norma's hand raised and landed on Ben's face with a stinging slap. "There," she said, spitting the words. "There! That's for being a stupid ape. That's for—"

The man stood there, looking at Margo, rubbed his cheek, and then drew himself up. He stood outlined against the cobalt sky, his dark head striking...and menacing.

Then he laughed, his eyes insolent. "What's the harm in a little kiss?" he demanded. "You're not nuns, are you?"

"Don't say another word if you know what's good for you," Margo cried. "Norma, come into the house."

She held out a hand and the girl took it. "Did he hurt you?"

"No. Let it go."

"If he did, he'll pay dear."

"But he didn't. Please. Just forget it."

They went into the house. "I'll have him thrown off the place," Margo said between her teeth.

"No, don't, *don't*. It was my fault. I was teasing him, the way he used to tease us. I should have known better. He has a trigger temper. He took the only revenge he knew. So...please, let it go. Just let it go. What am I, a sugar-plum fairy? I'm a grown woman, and I'm not afraid of Ben. Or anyone."

"I won't have him here any more."

"Then who'll do the gardening? You won't find anyone. Some kid, after school. They don't care. I said it was my fault. I did provoke him, I admitted that. I should have known better. Oh, don't spoil the whole evening, Margo. Come, let's water the plants upstairs. I haven't had time to do it for the last few days. They must be dying of thirst. Help me. That's the good girl."

They went up the stairs. "I knew he bothered you," Margo said stubbornly. "The first day I saw you talking to him. You looked disturbed. I won't have that."

At the top of the stairs Norma turned to her. There was a hardness in her face. "Listen to me, now," she said. "You just listen, Margo. I have to live in this town with him. He's a bit of a problem. But there are other problems, and I have to live with them too. There's no escape, the way there is in a large city. Here, you coexist. Ben lives here and so do I. So don't antagonize him. He won't forget it. You have to control someone like Ben, the way you have to control a computer. It's my business, not yours. Don't tell me how to run my life, Margo, I've managed so far without any help. I'm sorry you…I'm sorry you saw his pass. But it rolls off me, doesn't touch me. I have bigger problems than that."

She put a hand on Margo's elbow. "I mean it," she said. "Don't interfere."

"Wouldn't you do the same for me?"

"Not if I knew the circumstances."

"You mean to say, if someone attacked me the way he—"

"Don't try to play God," Norma said, with steel in her voice, and then, smiling her charming smile, put a hand through Margo's arm. "We are *not* going to talk about it any more," she said. "Now let's give the plants some water. We'll take turns."

On the balcony was a huge watering can which, when filled, bowed one down with the weight of it. There were four urns in all, gigantic iron pots filled with flowers of the season, at the moment marigolds and pansies and morning glories. Norma watered the first two and Margo the next, her arms aching with the effort. "That will do it for now," Norma said. "It's work, isn't it?"

"My God, yes."

"Ready for a stiff drink?"

"I want to wash a bit first."

"Then see you in short order," Norma said, putting the watering can back in its niche. "You must tell me about the tour. John said you seemed pleased with his performance."

"I was."

For dinner, spareribs and sauerkraut, and the candles flickering, and the breeze whispering through opened windows. Wine, in tall tumblers, and Pompey saying, "Seconds, for whoever wants them, otherwise we'll have leftovers tomorrow."

She was in her room at just before ten, and the telephone rang. She went to it warily, but it was only Douglas.

"I'd like your company tomorrow," he said.

"That sounds nice."

"Get here at around eleven and we'll find a nice place. I'm not sure but I think I know where."

"Yes, all right, fine, Doug."

"Don't oversleep."

"I'll have Pompey wake me."

"That's my girl."

When she was ready for bed she considered. Should she take the phone off the hook?

Better do, she decided, and removed it.

Then, half an hour later, went out again and put the receiver back on the hook. *Let's just see*, she thought.

But it didn't ring.

At first she was tense, waiting. Then dropped off, woke again, listening. And then slept once more.

Nothing woke her. In the morning she thought about it. Last night it hadn't rung. Why did it ring some nights and other nights didn't?

If I knew that, I'd know everything, she told herself, and put the riddle aside. Anyway, you never did know everything, nor would you if you lived to be a hundred. There were always imponderables. Life was like that…a guessing game.

•••

"How come you up and dressed so early today?" Pompey asked, looking up guiltily. He had been drowsing at the kitchen table.

"I'm going out to the farm again," she said.

"Again?" he repeated, looking too silly for words, like a fond mother or something.

"Any reason why not?" she asked.

"No reason I can think of," he said, and winked at her.

"Stop looking so ridiculous, Pomp."

"That the way I'm looking?"

"Darling, we grew up together."

He chuckled. "The boy next door."

"Not even that. In the same house."

"Brother and sister, like."

"Um hum."

He grinned. "You ain't fooling me."

"Could I have breakfast, please? That is, if you can stop smirking long enough to do me two eggs and bacon?"

"Ha ha," he laughed, and when she was ready to go, said earnestly, "joking aside, you're bound to end up in this neck of the woods, mark my words."

"Irritating," she said. "This morning you're *irritating*," but she kissed his leathery brown cheek and ran outside. In her car she headed for the north country road that led into the main highway. She passed Adams Crossing and then started to climb. It wasn't the steepest of ascents, but the townspeople referred to Blount's Hill as "the mountain." Not that there wasn't a lovely view, for there was, a broad outlook over field and valley and the geometric squares of sown land, colored according to their yields, pale mauves and delicious pistachios, and the golden tints of wheat waving in the breeze. For a moment she thought of the quiet acres of France, with their hedgerows and ancient white stone farmhouses and the rustic little churches with the golden crosses gleaming in the sun.

At the crest of the hill she slowed her engine and looked down, sniffing the country-scented air.

If she were in Europe now, there would be summit cafes, where one could look down over the beauty below and drink cold beer or thick coffee. American ways were different, alas and alack… there were no *gemutlich* bierstubes round about, no gossip and talk, only the sound of crows cawing in the winy air of a summer morning. *Well, never mind*, she thought and, taking her foot off the brake, started down the other side of the hill.

It was then that she heard the knock in the engine, puzzling… and new in origin. What was that? A click clack, click clack…and then a kind of dot dot, dash dash…like a Morse code.

What's wrong with this buggy? she asked herself, and going down the slope of the hill, gaining momentum, had a funny feeling.

A very funny feeling.

Because she was heading for a main highway on which would be a steady stream of cars, going fast…the speed limit was sixty-five miles an hour and, like as not, motorists in a hurry to get somewhere would be stepping it up to seventy or more, a wary eye out for motorcycle cops. If you wanted to make time, you made it on the highway, hoping to find a motel before dark. Or a roadside inn for lunch. Or a gas station where the kids could go to the john.

It was on the highways that death struck …

The knock in the engine became louder, *very* disturbing now, for she was nearing the bottom of the hill. Already she could hear the thunder of the cars below, the whine of tires on macadam, the occasional honk of a horn. Not far down, almost visible now, was the sign: COME TO FULL STOP.

But she didn't wait to reach that point; she braked.

Nothing happened.

The car continued to coast down, blithely careening along, like a mad thing which had taken matters into its own hands. What the hell, she muttered savagely, and stepped on the brake. There was no noticeable difference. She was heading hell-bent-for-leather for the highway below, powerless to stop the plunge.

For one scarifying, almost insane moment she thought about throwing open the door and jumping.

But not for long. She pictured the horrible consequences. In the hospital for months, her jaw wired, her limbs fractured, in traction…*It's not the answer*, her frenzied brain told her, and she swerved the car, only yards from the highway and, almost breaking her arms, wrenched the wheel with all the force she could muster. There was a scream of tires, the car danced on two wheels, and then headed for the brush and grass and trees at the side of the road. Rocking violently, as she clung to the wheel with desperate strength, it came to rest between two trees, shuddering like a bull elephant, and lodged there, choked by the elms and the hard, clumpy undergrowth of bush and tall grass and torn-up earth. The engine throbbed like a dirge as she opened the door and climbed out, wobbling on unsteady legs, and stood looking at the car, which was like some wounded beast in its death throes.

Now it will burst into flames, she thought, backing away. *Now it will die, be charred to cinders, poor thing, poor thing*…But instead the throbbing stopped, the motor died, and the little Impala, scratched but not wrecked, sat quiet and still, its tires tangled in leafy brush and moss. She left it, looking back once or twice, and plodded down the hill, standing with a finger up, and soon after was given a lift by a considerate motorist, who drove her to the gas station at Deer Crossing.

• • •

"My car's wedged between some trees," she told the boy who came toward her, wiping his hands on an oily rag. "Could you get it, please, and have my brakes checked? It's a second-hand car. I had no trouble with it until today. I nearly plowed into the rush of cars at the bottom of Blount's Hill, I would have been smashed to bits."

"Jaysus," he said, and opened the door of a little VW. "Hop in; we'll see what's what."

They drove back. The boy got out and opened the hood, fiddling inside. She smoked nervously. Then he came toward her, the slam of the hood echoing in the still air.

"Have to garage it for a day or two."

"What's wrong with it?"

"You try to be an auto mechanic?"

She was indignant. "I never touched the damned thing. I wouldn't know how! What are you trying to say?"

"Brakes loused up," he said tersely. "No doubt about it. Maybe a vandal. Anyway, there's work needs to be done."

"But I need a car."

"Two or three days," he repeated.

"Vandals," she said slowly. "You mean something was done to my car?"

"Sure was."

She got out and stood thinking. The telephone calls. Her brakes "loused up." And she was to sit idly by while —

"You're telling me that something was deliberately done to my brakes?" she asked.

"It's got to be that way, Ma'am."

"I see."

She lit another cigarette, puffed avidly, and then asked if she could rent a car.

"Yes, Ma'am. I'll have to speak to my captain, ask him how much."

"I don't care how much," she snapped. "Just rent me a car and charge me whatever the going cost is. Meanwhile, get this one into shape. I want a small car with good mileage, okay?"

"Okay," he said, and they drove back to the garage.

Ten minutes later she drove away in a little buff-colored Datsun. This might be God's country, but they had asked a stiff price. So what? Supposing she had been killed, come face to face with that thunderous traffic…there wouldn't have been enough left of her to put into a garbage bag.

She went on her way, grim-faced. Who had tampered with her brakes and why? It was not in her nature to be suspicious, and if it weren't for the telephone calls she might have settled for a matter of misfortune. Brakes could go bad and brakes did…anyone knew that, but "tampered with?"

Coldly calm now, she thought of the people she was involved with: John, Pompey, Norma, Jim Bach, Ed Corliss. Clara.

And then she laughed helplessly, trying to imagine one of those persons doing something nasty to her brakes.

It was just too ridiculous …

"It's just too ridiculous," she said to Douglas, when he banged the screen door behind him and came toward her across the lawn.

"What is?"

"Someone wrecked my car. I mean someone did something to the brakes. Behold this rented property. Mine is garaged for a day or two."

"Take it slow and easy," he said. "Get out, and we'll talk about it over drinks."

They sat in the kitchen, sipping. "I put my foot down but nothing happened," she said, with a delayed reaction. Her hand was barely able to hold the glass.

"Yes, and then what?"

"Why, death on the highway," she said. "Headed for the Great Beyond."

"Get that down you," he ordered.

"I'm drinking it."

"No, swallow it fast, and then another one."

"I hate a quick drunk," she complained, but already felt the haze settling over her, comforting, comforting.

"Here we go again, swallow, come on, swallow."

"I'll drown," she said.

"No you won't, drink."

"Yes, Douglas."

"That's the girl."

There was a silence, while they sat looking out the kitchen window. "What do you think?" she asked, after a while.

He turned away from the window and looked at her. "What do I think? I have some ideas, yes. Not fully formed yet, so I won't say."

"Give me a clue," she said, feeling the liquor.

"Do *you* have any ideas?"

"Ideas? What ideas? I can't imagine why I should be a target."

"Come come," he said impatiently. "You inherited the whole kit and kaboodle, didn't you?"

She stared at him. "You mean the house?"

"Some people would give their eye teeth."

She laughed. "But why for God's sake? There's no money to go with it! How can I make use of it? It was an empty gesture. I don't know why she did it."

"Okay, let it go for now. You're safe and sound, in one piece. Thank God for small and large favors. Come here, I want to feel you, sound and healthy as you are."

"I will certainly not go there," she said spiritedly. "If you want to feel for broken bones, don't bother, there aren't any."

"Well, *that* sounds like the old Margo," he replied, grinning, and got up. In front of her he crouched down, closing his eyes. "Stroke my forehead," he said. "I have a kind of nagging headache."

"Why didn't you say so? I'm sorry, Douglas."

"Just move your fingers back and forth. I love having you touch me."

She did that, and he knelt, letting her fingers move slowly back and forth on his forehead. "Nice," he murmured, and his head rested on her knees. After a while he said "Thank you, better now," and then, "Any idea who could have done something to your car?"

"Your guess is as good as mine."

"*My* guess is better than yours."

"What do you mean by that?"

He gave her a quick look and then got to his feet. "I know things you don't," he said. "There are a few facts I have to get sorted out in my mind, and when I do we'll talk more about this. Meanwhile, let's go to Rockville. There's a place called the Yellow Astor Inn. Okay, dearie?"

• • •

The Yellow Astor Inn was situated beside a small lake of purest blue, with ducks quacking stridently, and lovely overhanging old trees. They had shell steaks and a spinach salad, and the strawberry shortcake was the biscuit kind, the way upstate people made it. "You look better now," Douglas said.

"And fatter. What a meal."

"Let's drive back and I'll make fresh drinks."

"Doug, you have work to do."

"All work and no play makes Jack a dull boy."

So they drove back, and over whisky sours sat in the quiet, sunlit kitchen until the sun started to sink. Once Lucas came in and conferred with Douglas about some farm matter. When he went out Margo looked at the wall clock. "It's almost five," she said. "I must go. How about coming back with me, La Fayette? Have dinner with us again."

"I can't, not tonight," he said. "What did you call me?"

"Just a silly," she said. "Sure you won't share our meal tonight?"

"Are you falling for me?"

"You're not giving me much chance to, turning down my invitation."

"Would you, if I gave you a chance?"

"You don't really expect an answer to that?"

"You're not much help, are you?"

"So long for now," she said, giving his arm an affectionate pat, and getting into her car drove past the cross-bar fence, heading for home. When she pulled into the driveway, John was just climbing out of his own car. He glanced at the Datsun and lifted his eyebrows.

"Yes, it's a rented vehicle," she said.

"How come?"

"Mine had bad brakes. It's laid up for a few days."

"Oh, really?"

"Yes, really. First time I've *ever* had that kind of trouble."

"Oh, sorry," he said, frowning. *Why don't you ask me about it?* she thought, and shrank from the hand he had put on her elbow. After all, he could ask her what *happened* ...

The young assistant from the lawyer's office was just coming out the door, attache case under his arm.

"Good evening," he said.

"Day's work done, Ed?"

"Yes, sir," the young man answered.

"Coming along all right?"

"Not bad."

"Enjoy your evening."

"Thanks very much."

They went inside. "I'm off to the shower," John said. "Be down in two shakes."

"I'll skip drinks this evening," she said. "I have a nagging headache."

"Oh, sorry, anything I can do?"

"I'll take aspirins; they'll do the trick."

She didn't have a "nagging headache." She had simply seized on Doug's headache as an excuse. She didn't want to make small talk, she didn't want to drink with John, and for what reason she couldn't have said. Simply, she didn't *want* to, it was as plain as that. There was something tugging at her as well, a new thought, a strange, odd thought.

Ed Corliss.

He was a quiet young man, *too* quiet. An old-young man, with his attache case, his polite manner, his saying "sir" to John. There was something faintly distasteful about him. *Why? I don't know why*, she thought, *there just is.*

Take it from there, she thought, and took it from there. Ed Corliss was here from morning till night. He could have done something to her brakes.

For what reason?

For what reason had *anyone* done something to them?

• • •

There was still fifteen minutes to go before dinner. She ran down the stairs for a bottle to take up to her room. She would have her drink, alone, upstairs. She was just about to go up again when the door opened.

It was Norma, looking very lovely in a knit pants suit the color of apricots. She saw Margo and smiled radiantly. "Hi, here's the pest again," she said, and dropped her keys, a little self-consciously, into her handbag. "I hope you don't mind my letting myself in."

"Why should I? I'm glad to see you." She was cordial, happy that there would be a full dinner table, not just herself and John. "I'm skipping the cocktail hour, though, trying to get rid of a slight headache. See you shortly."

"Oh, do feel better."

"It's not much of a headache."

Well, there's no doubt about it, Margo thought, in her room. *Norma and John. Lovers. Letting herself into the house, a key at her disposal. But then I sensed it almost at once*, she thought, and smoked a cigarette, slowly changing into another dress after a quick bath. When it was seven, she went down again, and Pompey was standing at the foot of the stairs, calling for her. "Someone said you had a headache, Miss Margo?"

"It's gone."

"Fine," he said, "fine."

But it was not as festive as usual. She couldn't forget about that terrified flight down the hill, the car out of control, and the swish of cars at the bottom. She ate without appetite, and abruptly left the living room later to John and Norma, telling Pompey that she wanted to help with the dishes. She was clumsy, though, and succeeded in dropping a dinner plate, one of the blue Spode. He swept it up with a small brush.

"Don't worry," he told her. "Plenty more plates from this set. Two dozen and extras, just don't give it a thought. Belongs to you, anyways."

Norma marched into the kitchen. "What's this about your car?" she demanded.

"The…the brakes didn't work."

"John just told me. What happened?"

"They didn't work. I plowed into some trees. No harm done. Except my car's in repair, I rented another one."

"Margo, dear God!"

"I escaped unharmed, as you can see."

Pompey started flapping his arms around. "Why you didn't tell me this?"

"I would have. In due time."

"I can't *believe* it," Norma said.

"It happened, Norma. Benefit of some unfriendly person, who knows who."

"What do you mean, unfriendly person?"

"The mechanic said my brakes had been tampered with."

There was a moment of silence and then everyone started talking at once: John too had come in and was listening. At the word "tamper" there was bedlam, Pompey wringing his hands and Norma exchanging glances with John, and although there had been no headache before, there was one now. In fact, if she didn't get to bed soon, she would require first aid.

"Excuse me," she said, her forehead beading with perspiration. "I just want to sleep, if you don't mind. I'm really fatigued. It's been a long day, with a few puzzles and unfathomables. May I just go up to bed, please?"

"Get out of my way, just get out of my way," Norma said, brushing John aside. "Can't you see she's had enough? Let me help her, let me help her …"

"No, not even you, Norma," Margo said, the room swimming around her. "I'm okay, really okay, just leave me be. Just leave me be. That's bad grammar, but I can't think straight…only, let me alone, all of you, just let me alone."

At last in her room, the light fading, questions, questions, and flopping, like a fish, into the bed, covers hastily drawn down. She burrowed into the pillows, while a cold, still voice whispered into her ear, and demonic laughter rang out, and her temples throbbed with excruciating pain. *Now I know*, she thought, in the purple light of a dying summer evening. *Now I know.*

Someone here wanted her to die.

Someone.

Someone …

CHAPTER TEN

Aunt Vicky was calling her.

"Help, Margo…help…please help …"

The voice faded away.

Turning, Margo sighed.

In her sleep, she brushed a fly away from her face.

"Margo …"

Now, listen, Aunt Vicky was calling, you heard that, didn't you?

There was that frightful struggle to pull out of sleep; there were nets around her; her feet were in sand. There was a cloud across her face; ropes binding her arms.

"Ugh," she moaned, wrestling, trying to unbind herself.

Something's wrong. Her mind, waking slowly, acknowledged it. *Something's wrong.*

Trouble, there was trouble, she had to do something; Aunt Vicky was calling out. The fear woke her up, the terrible fear.

Aunt Vicky wasn't dead. She was in the fruit cellar, where they had buried her under the coal heap, and she was choking in soot …

I'm coming, a part of her mind cried, but she couldn't work her way out of this thick fog…there was no life left in her. That was because they had covered her up with sand, first her feet, then her legs, her arms, torso …

Laughing, they filled a bucket of sand, held it poised. Laughing.

"Not my face," she cried, her eyes bulging, and then they upturned the bucket and it was in her nose and mouth and finally her eyes. There was nothing left after that: she was dead too, under the silver-white sand, they would never find her there. Not for years and years.

Her blood bubbled up from under the sand.

"Look at that," one of them said. "Those pretty red bubbles, oh, what fun …"

Her eyes snapped open.

Her heart was pounding like a trip hammer. The taste of brass was in her mouth. It was blood, she thought at first, but that was only the dream. The taste was disgust, revulsion, the abhorrence of a sick dream.

She turned on her back and put a hand over her clamorous heart. *How awful*, she thought, *how awful. What puts this garbage into our minds?*

And then there was something that was not a dream. Not dream, but reality. She was fully awake now, and she heard it clearly. A voice from downstairs, faint but distinct.

"Help …"

Aunt Vicky was dead, it wasn't Aunt Vicky. It was Pompey. Pompey …

What were they doing to him?

"I'm coming, I'm coming," she cried, springing out of bed. "Just a second…I'm coming …"

Pompey …

She grabbed a robe, shoveled into it, not bothering to tie the sash. There was that eerie voice, pleading.

Dashing out, she raced down the hall. Light came fitfully from the windows at either end, just a vapor of light, but she saw the stairs, and she listened.

Once more, a wisp of sound, the voice came.

And then she acted.

Put her foot on the first step, for guidance, and then started down. She was mumbling. "I'm coming, don't worry, don't worry …"

If Pompey's going to die I won't be able to stand it, she thought, her eyes trying to plumb the darkness. I couldn't bear that. Oh, please …

Halfway down there was a snake. The snake coiled around her legs, malevolent and evil, and, sucking in her breath, she knew that this time it was the end. Words came to her mind, words not even part of her faith…"Holy Mary, Mother of God …"

Then thought vanished and she plunged down the stairs, like someone shot out of a cannon.

For seconds, perhaps minutes, there was only numbness, of the mind and spirit. As for her body, she felt every bone, every tendon. She was stunned, dazed, knew it, tried to function properly, failed to do so, and lay in the thick, silent dark sucking her tongue, into which she had bitten. Slowly, lethargically, she raised a finger to her mouth.

It came away wet.

And sticky.

She was never sure how long she lay there, carefully feeling herself, moving cautiously. She knew at once that there were no bones broken. You broke a bone, you didn't have to guess about it. She did know that she had massive bruises, that she would be stiff for days and, as for tennis, forget it. When she finally pulled herself up she was flaming with pain, crying with the anguish of it.

God help me, was her next thought, and then, *Who did this terrible thing to me?*

She groped her way to the Long Room, found a lamp and switched it on. Then she went out to the hall again and snapped on a light there, looked up the stairs. She knew the snake was a figment of her imagination. There was no snake.

And then she saw what had tripped her up.

A length of twine, tied to one side of the banister halfway up the stairs, hanging free now, but that was because she had dislodged it from its mooring, for it had been strung across the stairwell, like a booby trap, from one side of the banister to the other.

I must have a charmed life, she thought and, pale and shaking, saw that what had almost killed her was a length of the twine

Ed Corliss was ticketing the historic pieces with that filled Brand Manor. There was no doubt at all: it was the same, identical twine that encircled desks and tables and lamps and sofas, ending in little, neatly-lettered tags…*Hitchcock lamp, circa* 1729…*See page* 21 *in the catalogue* …

She stood weaving, blurry-eyed.

And Ed Corliss had his own key …

With a sudden murderous compulsion, she dragged herself to the stairs and yanked the cord away from its mooring. Then she crept painfully down again and dropped it conspicuously on the living room rug. *I want it to be seen*, she thought, half out of her mind. *Let whoever has done this infamous thing see it, and know.*

She looked at it, and it was suddenly as lethal as the snake she had thought of. It was evil, that bit of twine, worse than the most poisonous cobra. The mind that had stretched it across the stairs was a hideous mind. That someone could think up such a heinous thing …

She turned out the lamp in the Long Room. It was suddenly imperative to get back to bed. Pain made her nauseated; she was rocking on her heels. One minute more and she might keel over.

In the dark, fumbling, she turned. The light from the hall was sixty watts, feeble, in a small tole lamp. She stumbled against a table, muttered a half-crazed imprecation, and it was then that the fear came, the terrible fear.

Because someone had been down here, calling up.

"Help … "

Someone who knew the workings of her mind. That she would think of Pompey. Someone clever and intelligent. Death was in her mind, because she had walked into a house of recent death. Pompey was an old man. Instinctively, without thought, she had rushed down because of Pompey.

And this person had taken that into account, had guessed her reactions.

I could have been smashed beyond recognition, she thought, my neck broken, my spine fractured. There was a good chance that it could have been that way, a better than even chance.

And someone had hoped for the worst.

It was at that moment that she heard the sound.

Just a breath of sound. Faint, like the rattle of paper…like material brushing past a chair, like fabric chafing against fabric.

The hair rose on her head.

And then…and then …

It came to her, like a thunderbolt, that whoever had called up those dark stairs would be here now. Would have to be here, unless he had gone out the back door, and that would be easily heard in the quiet. She was not alone.

Someone was here, near her.

Very near.

How she got up those stairs again, her body battered as it was, she never knew. What saved her was that her eyes had become accustomed to the darkness, and the faint moonlight, and the fact that she knew every turn and corner and nook and cranny and unexpected round and squiggle of the old house. She streaked out of the Long Room, hurtling up the steps two at a time, dashed down the upper corridor to her room, flung the door shut, leaned against it panting and gulping, shaking uncontrollably.

There was someone downstairs.

She cried tears of pain, sagged, gritting her teeth.

But there was someone downstairs …

There was no specific area where she hurt. She hurt all over.

But there was someone downstairs …

She listened for a sound, pressing her ear to the door. She stayed there, patient, hoping for something tell-tale, give-away… and remembered a childhood horror story about two people on opposite sides of a door. The victim hearing the sinister breathing, faint with fright, listening to the dread breath of a murderer …

She heard nothing. The house was as silent as a tomb.

Finally she left her post, went into the bathroom, ran a hot tub, a half-way measure for wrenched muscles. She lay in it, kneading her legs and arms and rubbing the worst bruises with her fingers.

There was no sense in trying to dry herself; the perspiration was dripping off her. She wrapped herself in a towel, lit a cigarette and paced the room, thinking. It was difficult to concentrate, but she must, she must …

Ed Corliss, then. *His* twine.

He came and went on his job, had a key. And that soft, eerie sound downstairs, like the breathing over the telephone.

It seemed fantastic that this polite, perhaps over-polite young man would want harm to come to her. What could possibly be his reason? And yet she didn't know all the facts…there might be something she couldn't even guess at.

If Ed Corliss, to hazard a guess, stayed up half the night in order to make intimidating phone calls, he would also be capable of quietly driving out to Brand Manor and letting himself in just as quietly and then rigging up that trap on the staircase. If you could do one rotten thing, you could do another rotten thing.

But, she thought, *there is also John.*

John wouldn't have to resort to devious measures, such as parking a car outside, making sure the front door was closed without waking a household, wary lest a key scrape in the lock.

Because John lived here.

She felt a fluttering in her chest. Yes, and John had lived here always…all his life, more or less. Like Pompey, it was his home. He had been loved and cosseted, his shirts ironed by Pompey's sister, Clara; he had had the best of all possible worlds for years and years and years.

And now he was threatened with eviction, or something very close to it, should she, Margo, choose to take over the house for herself.

Take it further, she thought. Suppose he was seething with discontent, rebellion, anger, fury…suppose he had taken a length of Ed Corliss' twine, rigged it up on the stairs, thus throwing suspicion on Ed, and then, downstairs in the dark, called up, simulating her aunt's voice?

Insane as the supposition seemed, it was logical enough. Desperate people did desperate things. Had it been John downstairs, in the horrible dark…waiting until she went upstairs again, when his plan had misfired …

Or …

A chill went through her.

Or had he been stealthily moving toward her to finish her off? Take a heavy object and smash in her skull?

And leave the front door open, so that it would be thought an intruder had entered, and done the foul deed.

And had he tampered with her brakes?

Even in a small town there were marauders…no place was totally safe these days. The garage boy had talked about vandals. Yes, and if there were vandals there could also be murderers. So that John—if it was John—could have a point. And in the morning, when Pompey wakened him, telling him about the ghastly event in the night, he could rush downstairs, hold a hand to his mouth, raise a fist in anger, revulsion and shock.

Anyone could be a good actor if it meant his own safety and security.

She lit another cigarette, patting at her damp face with a tissue. She was trying to remember the terms of the will. Let's see…the will said that if she, Margo, didn't choose to live at Brand Manor, the house then went to the Historical Society. So what would John's case be?

He couldn't win either way. If she accepted the gift of the house, he lost. If she refused, he lost. Then why would he try to do harm to her? *Nothing makes any sense*, she told herself, and sat down. It hurt. She walked, and it hurt. She lay down, and it hurt.

Let's face it, I feel awful, she thought. *It's terrible to feel so badgered, so hounded, and a solid ache from top to toe, to boot.* Angry tears sprang to her eyes. Why should she have to endure this lonely pondering…*why?*

She pounded a fist on a table.

Why?

A new pain flamed through her, as the self-inflicted blow sent shivers up from palm to shoulder. A new pain…and this one cleared her brain. There was a brilliant flash of insight.

Why, naturally, she thought, reaching for another cigarette. *Why, naturally!*

John.

John, should the house revert to the Historical Society, would almost certainly be named curator. Any reason why not? None. Yet every reason why he should be, considering his knowledge of the house's history, his long tenure in it, his lifetime association with its owner, Victoria Brand.

Certainly the house couldn't be left untenanted. In which case it was only reasonable that John would go on living here. It would add to his stature. He would be better off than he had ever been while Aunt Vicky was alive.

And the telephone calls. John hadn't heard them? Only a floor above her and he hadn't heard them? Suppose he had *made* them, quietly dialing the number of the phone, one story below… and then, perhaps smiling, a hand over his mouth and the other dashing back his thick, dark hair, listened to her impassioned protestations, meanwhile breathing into the instrument …

She went to the door and listened. Utter quiet, not a sound, not a breath. She turned on another lamp. Oh, if there were only *locks* on the doors! But there were only tongue-in-groove latches in these old, old houses. Very pretty, very decorative, but no protection against intruders in the night.

And anyway, say there *was* a lock on her door…there was no such thing as a foolproof lock, and John had lived in this house since boyhood. Doubtless he had access to every room in the place. *So it's come to that; I'm afraid of him*, she thought, *afraid of what he might do next…or if not him, then, for God's sweet sake*, who?

She lay awake, every nerve strained.

But the telephone didn't ring that night.

CHAPTER ELEVEN

In the morning she could scarcely get out of bed.

I can't, she thought flatly. The slightest move was agony. She rolled over slowly, and just as slowly raised herself. She *had* to get up. The worst thing, under the circumstances, was to lie in bed. Get the circulation started, that was the ticket.

The first few hours would be the hardest.

"Okay, okay," she said aloud, and eased herself up. "It's only exquisite pain; who cares about a little pain?"

Somehow she was able to sponge her body; reaching her back was the worst, and at one point she thought she might pass out. She sat down on the edge of the tub and put her head between her knees. And when she was finished with her ablutions tossed off a brandy from the bottle she had brought up last night.

It helped.

She pulled on blue jeans, got into a shirt, dabbed on some cologne, went to the bathroom and did her eyes nicely, and went down the stairs cautiously, holding on to the railing. Pompey saw her slow progress into the kitchen. "What's your trouble?" he asked.

"I fell down last night."

His eyes popped. "You did *what?*"

"I thought I heard you calling me in the night, and I started down and then fell the rest of the way."

He stared at her. "I don't sleep downstairs," he said, his mouth hanging open.

"I know that!"

"Then what you mean?"

"Someone was downstairs, calling out, someone crying for help."

"Now this I gotta get straight," he said, sitting her down in a chair.

"Don't sit me down so *fast*," she said, wincing.

"All right now?"

"All right, you say? Lord, I can't find a comfortable position, there *is* no comfortable position. But I'm all right, don't you fret. I don't know why, but I am."

"Now you talk. What happened?"

"I woke up. I had a horrid dream and I woke up from it and heard someone calling me. It was the reason for the dream, I imagine. I must have heard that voice and in my sleep was uneasy."

"And then?"

"I could hear someone saying 'Help.' "

"Who?"

"First I thought it was Aunt Vicky and then I thought it was you."

"What would I be doing downstairs in the middle of the night?"

"I was half asleep! I heard the voice downstairs and I didn't stop to think. I just wanted to get down there, and help you."

His voice was soft. "Thanks, dearie, thanks, Miss Margo. All right, so you went downstairs, crazy girl…and then?"

"And then there was an obstacle. It tripped me up. I fell all the rest of the way down those long stairs."

"What kind of obstacle?"

"A length of twine. Stretched across from one banister to the other. I fell over it and plunged to the bottom."

"Twine?" he repeated, and she saw his instant comprehension.

"Yes, the kind Ed Corliss uses."

He sat down, his face dark and forbidding, looked at her, finally slapped a palm on the table. "This here is what you are going to do," he said. "Go away for a spell. Stay with Mr. Douglas. These telephone calls and me supposed to be calling you from downstairs.... There's danger here, I can't hardly believe it, but there is. Why, I'd like to—"

He turned purple: she was really alarmed.

"I sleep like a log," he shouted. "Calling from downstairs…me? I got nothing on my conscience, I can sleep, which is more than some people can say."

"Some people?" she asked curiously. "About whom are you talking, Pompey?"

"Just never mind," he said grimly. "I got something to think about. Some ideas, you just let me work them out. Now you eat your eggs and shut up. I don't want to hear another word from you until you finish that there breakfast."

He left her and came back a few minutes later. "Mr. Doug is stopping by in a half hour or so," he said. "Here, drink some more coffee. Then get yourself dressed. I told him what happened."

"You called Doug, you shouldn't have done that," she said edgily.

He answered, "I do what I'm called on to do. Now you scoot up and put some clothes on, you hear?"

They drove hither and yon, stopping off once for coffee and pie. Doug kept saying, "Tell me again, and don't leave out anything."

"I told you."

"Tell me again."

"I had the dream and when I woke up I heard someone calling out for help. It was Pompey, I thought. So I went to the stairs and then there was the rope, the twine."

"And while you were still downstairs you heard a sound?"

"Yes, there was someone there."

"You *thought* there was someone there."

"No. There *was* someone there."

"Are you in much pain?"

She was able to laugh now. "Let's say I've felt better in my life."

"I don't want you staying in that house," he said. "I'll take you back and then you put some things in a bag and stay with me at the farm."

"I'm not leaving," she said quietly.

"Now you listen to me …"

"No. I'm not leaving. Only now I won't take any chances, that much I've learned. And the telephone can ring forever, so far as I'm concerned."

"What does that mean?"

She looked away. "I guess I didn't tell you about that."

Patiently, he put both arms on the table. "Tell me now," he said. "And if there's anything else, tell me that too."

"There's nothing else, just that."

She explained. "The first night, though, I was too weary to really have it register. And then the second night, and the next night. So I started leaving the receiver off the hook, sometimes, anyway."

"And you didn't think to say anything about it before this?" he asked, snapping a muddler in two.

"There was one furtive moment when I thought it might be you," she admitted, and he flushed.

"*Me?*"

"I thought of everything," she said calmly. "And I thought of that too."

There was a rather long silence.

"I won't apologize," she said. "From the minute I came here unpleasant things began to happen. As I said, I had to think of everything…and everyone."

He finally turned back to her. "I'm sorry," he said. "I can see how you might have thought something like that. You never thought it again, did you?"

"No."

"You're sure?"

"I'm sure."

He reached over for her hand. She gave it willingly enough. He stroked it and kissed it and then gave it back. "More coffee?" he asked.

"Thanks, no."

"All right, what would you like to do?"

"Something I haven't done yet, it wasn't the right time," she said. "But now it *is* the right time. If it's all right with you, Douglas, I'd like to visit her grave."

"You're sure you're up to it?"

"Yes, quite sure."

"Then, fine. We'll stop for some flowers along the way. I usually patronize De Nyse; they know just about what I want."

"Do you go often?"

"No rules and regulations about it. Whenever I can spare the time. I'm not a pious sort of guy, and she wouldn't want it to be out of duty."

He added, as they stood up, "She'd be glad, whenever someone had the chance, of a visit. That house was always open, you never had to schedule an appointment. I think it should be the same now. Drop over whenever the opportunity arises, not because it's expected."

• • •

It was a simple enough headstone, in the old family plot. Generations of Brands were buried here in this green earth, and if she so wished, so would Margo be, perhaps next to her father, Thomas Brand, the grandson of James Brand, who had fathered Victoria and Edward and whose seed had led, irrevocably, to the birth of a girl named Margo. Cemeteries in the large cities might be crammed to the last foot of earth, but here there was room to spare for others to come, for eons, perhaps. She looked at the names: Benjamin, Nathaniel, James, Lavinia, Arria, Lucinda. It was a little city of the dead, with small children struck down in their infancy lying beneath tiny mounds like caterpillar tracks. They slept peacefully, all of them, giving their dust to enrich the earth, one with the ages.

VICTORIA BRAND, the headstone read. BORN 1890, DIED 1973. BELOVED DAUGHTER OF JAMES AND SOPHRONIA BRAND. INTEGER VITA, IN SEMPERTINA SAECULA.

They arranged the flowers, magenta and white peonies with a potent scent. Then they went to the font for water. "They'll last for a day or two," Douglas said. "They look nice, don't they?"

"They look beautiful, perfectly beautiful."

They sat for a while, listening to the quiet, and then got in the car again and drove off. "Home," Margo said, when he questioned her. "You have things to do, and I guess I'd like to be alone."

"But you won't be morbid?"

"No," she said earnestly. "Everything has to die, I quite understand that." And as he headed the car toward Brand Manor, she was remembering.

Integer vita.

A life of integrity.

In sempertina saecula.

To Him be glory evermore.

CHAPTER TWELVE

They had their picnic, Norma arranging it in her efficient fashion, phoning Doug, a cocktail in her hand, the evening before. "You are not to be late," she said concisely. "Be here at ten, and no excuses."

"Men are so *dilatory*," she claimed, hanging up the phone. "I don't trust Doug, but then I don't trust any man, and never have."

Pompey packed a lunch, sandwiches with ham and cheese filling, roast beef and chicken. There were artichoke hearts and olives, plum tomatoes, potato salad. John made a pitcher of martinis, pouring it into a thermos.

They went in two cars, John with Norma and Margo with Douglas. It was a magnificent day, all gold and blue and balmy, with the lake rippling gently, the sun like fire. They swam and rested, talked idly. At one they sampled Pompey's basket, eating with appetite, and then uncorked the thermos of martinis. They had brought along a deck of cards, played gin rummy and then Casino.

It brought back the long-distant past, their common childhood, and filled her with nostalgia. When they tired of the card games she fell asleep, sated with food, fresh air, and the drinks. She dozed off, lying on her tummy in the sun, and when she woke the day had turned to late afternoon, with violet tints and birds twittering before their night's roosting.

How quiet it is, she thought, *how immensely quiet. Like an island in the mind's imagination, scarcely real at all.*

She had an abrupt sensation of being all alone in the world. A strange, eerie feeling, not peaceful or cozy, but somber, forlorn. She quickly turned over onto her back and raised her head.

She wasn't alone.

John was there, in his swim trunks, with his head turned away from her as he gazed out at the peacock-blue lake. She didn't say anything right away, just continued to watch him, with his tanned body and dark, rebellious hair. He seemed to be looking at something she was unable to see.

Where were the others, she wondered…why were she and John alone…and why did that fact disturb her, alert her? At that moment he turned, and their eyes met. There was a long, strange silence.

Then she collected herself. "Where are they?" she asked.

"Gathering driftwood for a fire," he answered.

"Oh?"

For some reason her lips were dry. She didn't like being alone with John. Reasoning with herself, she remembered that she and John had been children together; then why did she feel this profound distress at their proximity? This was John, John Michaels…what was *wrong* with her?

As if he sensed her unease, he bent and plucked a cattail from the moist ground. He held it for a moment and then, deliberately, and with malice aforethought, made a little loop in the stem and popped the head off.

The plumy, dry head went spinning.

It was a nihilistic act.

She thought of the guillotine and the garroe, looked away quickly as he plucked another cattail from the loamy ground. She heard the faint pop as the head spun off. The silence between them grew…and grew…and for the life of her she couldn't think of one single thing to say. Befuddled, she slipped on her dark glasses and looked at her toes, pink-tipped with Elizabeth Arden Angel Blush, and another head popped off.

"Hey there, we've got the makings of a roaring fire," Norma's voice cried, and she and Doug came around a dune, brandishing armloads of driftwood.

The uneasy, dark moment passed, and they took another swim, splashing, and when night finally fell, made the fire. The sparks flew and it was very pretty. A seagull glided down and picked at their leavings, giving them aggressive looks, and soon darkness was complete.

They sang softly, draining the pitcher of martinis. The "Wide Missouri," "Galway Bay," "Careless Love." The lake water beat against the bank. The stars came out and the moon, three quarters full, was their only light as they gathered up their gear and made their way to the parked cars.

They drove back, John leaving Norma at her flat and Douglas dropping Margo off at Brand House. "Better use some Noxema on that sunburn," he advised her, and tried to kiss her, but she evaded him. "It's late, Douglas."

"You can sleep, I can't. I don't care, however. Why do you shy away?"

"See you soon," she said, climbing out of the car.

"Afraid of me or of yourself?"

She ran up the stone steps to the porticoed veranda. "Night night, Douglas; it was a heavenly day."

She went on up, took the phone off the hook, brushed her teeth and crawled into bed. *Today I was a child again*, she thought, and then, dozing off, amended it. *No, a grown woman with a child's memories.* Almost asleep, there was a sharp, disturbing recollection…something about the lake, when they were little… some ugly, distressing recall that bothered her, nagged at her… something horrid, and quickly put aside, but not quite buried.

I must try to dig it out of my subconscious, she told herself, and then drifted off into nothingness, remembering the lovely day that had just passed but also remembering—or trying to—another day, another not very nice day. *Now, what was that*, she thought, in an attempt to call into being what her mind had repressed once long ago. *I must pin it down*, she thought earnestly, and then, spinning into sleep, forgot it. After all, she had forgotten other things …

•••

She woke early. The morning was bright and clear. Dew on the grass tipped the blades with brilliance. *I love the sun*, Margo thought, and dressed for church. "Just toast and coffee," she told Pompey. "I'm going to Mass."

"Mass?" he said wonderingly. "You was raised a Protestant, Miss Margo."

"Yes, I know, but I'm going to noon Mass."

"Heathen rites," he muttered, but fed her, and then she went off to the little Anglican church with the lily window and the red door, and knelt when the others knelt, took the wafer and sipped the wine. The organ thundered out liturgical music. "Please come again," the young, frocked priest said at the door, the sun slanting in and gilding his sandy hair. "I was so sorry to hear about your aunt's death."

"How kind of you," she said.

She walked all the way home, as she had walked there, for the day was cool and dry, and the exercise was what she had been wanting. In her mind was the majesty of the organ, and the ancient rites of the service of Mother Church. Protestant or no, it had all begun with what Pompey called heathen rites. Reciting to herself:

> *Hail, oh hail true Body*
> *Of the Virgin Mary born*
> *On the Cross thy sacred Body*
> *For us men with nails was torn.*
> *Cleanse us by thy Blood and Water*
> *Streaming from thy Pierced Side*
> *Feed us with thy Body broken*
> *Now and in death's agony …*

The walk back was quiet and peaceful. She thought, *I'll spend the day taking more pictures of the house* and, reaching it, saw Norma's car parked there, caught a glimpse of Ben Blough weeding round a fruit tree, and ran into John in the central hall, coming down the stairs in a bathrobe, shaved and immaculate and tossing back his dark hair. "I'm about to have brunch," he said. "How about keeping me company?"

She said fine, and that Norma was somewhere about, and they could all sit down together. "Where's Norma?" she asked, when Pompey came out of the kitchen.

"In the garden, picking flowers, of course."

"Well, I'll just get her in. John said something about brunch."

"Everything's ready; you got home just in time, my fair lady."

He had made wheat cakes; there was "genuine Vermont maple syrup, ladies and gentlemen." Also crisp bacon and buttermilk biscuits. The coffee was strong and piping hot.

"This is the life," John said lazily, and went back upstairs to get dressed. "What are you up to?" Norma asked.

"I'll do some photographing. Homework, you understand."

"Busy little bees, aren't we," Norma commented. "I have the whole house to do, flower-wise, Sunday's the day I can really get at it."

"And I'll wash up these here dishes," Pompey said, starting to clear the table. "I'll help," Margo said, and then the doorbell rang and Pompey made a resigned face. "Callers," he said. "I got to start making a new pot of coffee, looks that way to me."

"Never mind, I'll handle it," Norma said, looking over her shoulder at Margo. "I was told you went to All Souls. They'll have found out and I'm afraid you're in for it, my pet. As Pompey said, heathen rites ..."

Her voice trailed off.

But it wasn't the Ladies Aid.

"Mr. Zeiss is here," Norma announced, coming back with a funny little grin.

"Mr. Who?"

"Mr. Zeiss."

"Who's that?"

"He's from Manhattan and wants to take a look at the house."

"Oh, I see. John warned me about the sensation-seekers. Does he have credentials? John said—"

"As to that," Norma said, "I wouldn't know. He certainly does have a build like an ox. How he ties his shoelaces is more than I can fathom. He couldn't bend to find a lost collar button if it meant his very life. It's a mystery to me how he sees his feet at all. He looks pregnant, if you know what I mean." She waved a hand airily. "He's all yours, my dear, go and talk to him. Ask him to show you his credentials. All I know is he has a belly that would fill Proctor Hall, where we have our yearly concerts."

There was no way to signal Norma that the person in question had ambled into the room and was now standing, leaning against a doorframe, listening with interest. At Norma's last phrase he smiled amicably, patted the belly just mentioned, and nodded.

"Furthermore," he said, while Norma turned sharply, a hand over her mouth, "I *do* have credentials, as you shall soon see."

"Oh, I *do* beg your pardon," Norma said, scarlet, and fled.

"I'm Abner Zeiss," the stranger said, holding out a beefy hand. "You're Miss Brand?"

"Yes...my friend didn't mean anything ..."

"I'll forgive a beautiful woman anything," he said cheerfully. "Two beautiful women in a single day is almost more than a man can bear. Sit down and I'll show you my credentials. I'd rather show you my etchings, but it's neither the time nor the place. I see you've been feeding on something. Is there anything left for a hungry man?"

"Yes, I'm sure...Pompey?"

"Just coffee," Mr. Zeiss said genially, seating himself. "And some pie or whatever, blueberry muffins? Of course I'm very partial to rhubarb pie; you wouldn't have any of that, would you?"

"Gotta settle for wheat cakes," Pompey said, not a bit put out. "Set down and make yourself at home. Give him some coffee, Miss Margo, I be right back." His glance was respectful. "You got a lot there to feed," he said, surveying the stranger's bulk. "Seems to me I better make a second batch."

Afterwards Margo thought, *I took to Abner Zeiss right away, and so did Pompey.* "That's a gentleman and a scholar," he told her, when Mr. Zeiss had left at about four in the afternoon. "You tell him to come around any time, he fits in here just fine."

• • •

But before Abner Zeiss left in midafternoon, he had done several things. Number one, shown his credentials, bringing out a great mass of impressive-looking cards from a shabby traveling wallet. In no time at all Margo learned that he was an M.D. (OB-Gyn).

"But that's only to pay the rent," he said hastily. He was also an authority on pre-Columbian art, on Chinese dynasty culture, a writer, lecturer, professor, philosopher, psychologist, philatelist.

"A Renaissance man," Margo said, dazzled. He was in his sixties, and when he stood up, after thanking Pompey for the food, he reminded Margo of Moses, with his spiky white hair like something sculpted out of stone, his heavy-lidded statue eyes, and his enormous frame with the protuberant belly. Moses holding up the tablets…THOU SHALT NOT KILL…

Moses, to be sure, with a Bronx accent, nasal and heavily dentalized. He wasn't more than five feet ten or eleven, but he looked like a giant, and it didn't take much imagination to picture him saying, "Fee fi fo fum, I smell the blood of an Englishman …"

He asked to be shown around the house. "I showed you my credentials," he reminded her.

"Oh, John does that," she said. "Tour day is Wednesday."

"I don't mean a *tour*," he said impatiently. "I just want to see what you've got here."

"Then, shall I call John? He's gone upstairs to dress."

"What's the matter with you? I like your looks, you're a tasty young thing. I'd prefer to have you take me about."

Later, he teased her about it. "You gave me the tour," he told her, "in spite of yourself. I never loved you more."

Because, walking through the rooms, the words, Aunt Vicky's words, came back to her. She was scarcely conscious of what she was saying. "Who were these travelers who chose this as their final home? They were the terminal off-shoot of a body of emigrants organized in England in 1629, largely through the exertions of ...

"You see this view from the window, Mr. Zeiss? Early in the morning of September 8, 1795, Colonel Trueheart led his men on a scouting mission. They assembled right there, near the large double elm. High hearts and high hopes...but they were ambushed by the Indians on the shores of a little pond known to us now as Bloody Point, and most of the men were killed, including the officers ...

"Jonathan's son became a successful sea captain. His name was Benjamin Brand. Many of the treasures in this house come from his travels. This platter on the Dutch sideboard, the plates in the cupboard, the pewter and brass, the candlesticks. And jewelry brought back from St. Petersburg for his wife: earrings and rings and bracelets."

"Bravo," Mr. Zeiss said, when they had come full circle back to the central hall again. "Bravo. What have we got to drink?"

"Sherry? Bourbon? Whatever you wish," she said, and they sat in the Long Room, talking for another hour. He invited her to lunch the next day. "Call you in the morning," he said nasally. "You have a car?"

"I got it back only a few days ago," she said. "They told me a few days, but it was more like a week."

"Oh. What was the trouble?"

"Bad brakes."

"So?" he commented, and she found herself telling him about it. "Down the hill, and the brakes didn't work. Tampered with, he said, the boy from the garage. Vandals, he said. But I didn't quite buy that."

"Someone put a hex on you?" Mr. Zeiss suggested. "This is hex country; I'm sure you know that."

"I don't think a hex can bollux up brakes," she said, and he grinned.

"The Devil moves in his mysterious ways his wonders to perform," he murmured.

"That's sacrilege, isn't it?"

"No. God and the Devil are one. Or were one at a certain time."

He drove off in a rather battered Cutlass station wagon, with a great crack in the front windshield. The house was quiet and golden, the trees outside trembling gently, and she sat there on a sofa, remembering one of the last things he had said.

"So you don't know what to do about this house? I'll tell you what you'll do. You'll live here and love living here. You'll end your days here, like your aunt, or great-aunt, or great-great aunt or whatever she was."

"Could you tell me how I'd manage that?"

"What's that mean?"

"I'm only a poor working girl. Or, better, not even that yet. Who's going to pave the way?"

"There will be a way," he said imperturbably. "You'll find a way."

"Mr. Zeiss, there's no money at all!"

"Money," he cried, his lip curling. "Money! Have a little faith, for God's sake."

"In what, miracles?"

"There have always been miracles. Ask my people, they'll tell you. We were slaves in Egypt. And the Red Sea parted for us. Miracles? We can tell you about miracles."

He drove off, majestic, Moses without the staff. "Don't forget about lunch tomorrow," he called, rolling down the car window. "I'll phone you in the morning, soon as I find an interesting place."

"Yes, fine," she said, and waved as he crackled down the pebbled way to the road below.

Pompey had a lovely little Sunday supper for them later. Boston baked beans and boiled ham, salad, chocolate swirl cake for dessert. "Alas, to the salt mines on the morrow," Norma said at ten, and drove off. One more lovely day had slipped by, all blue and pink and gold, scented with Norma's flowers. *I'm marking time*, Margo thought. *What will I eventually do?*

The telephone rang in the night. She hopped up, trembling, spoke. "It's you, isn't it, Ben? I know it's you. Now I know. It's you, Ben."

But there was only the silence, except for the quiet breathing, and she banged the phone down. Another sleeping pill. Lying tense, waiting for it to do its work. The phone rang again and she lay there, willing the drug to do its work, which it finally did, and she didn't care, it was as simple as that; she was three quarters asleep. It rang again and she laughed. "Go to hell," she said. "I can't be bothered."

He didn't bargain for that, she thought. He didn't bargain for that ...

Pompey called her in the morning. "It's that man," he said. "The one with the funny shape. Want to speak to him?"

"Yes, I do," she said, and hopped out of bed.

"Mr. Zeiss?"

"Call me Abner," he said. "Hello, there's a Greek place in town, name of Linardos, meet me there at one."

"I know the place, I'll be there," she said, and got herself together, bathing and dressing.

"Just fruit juice and coffee," she told Pompey.

"You trying to starve yourself?"

"No, I'm lunching with Mr. Zeiss," she said. "I can't eat a regular breakfast and lunch too."

"You wanta end up a TB case?"

"Oh, Pompey," she said, and drove away, making good time, parking on State Street, where the Greek place was.

"So here you are," Abner Zeiss said, his mouth full of *pita* bread. "You'll have ouzo, gotta keep everything in character."

They had ouzo, and then gorged on *moussaka*, finishing up with thick coffee and *baklava*. Ashes, from Abner's gargantuan cigar, dribbled down onto his lapels. He regaled her with anecdotes, told her she was a damned pretty girl, and was treated royally by the proprietor. Not only that, several persons stopped at his table, wanting to shake his hand. "Let's get married," Margo said, charmed with him. "Where have you been all my life?"

He said he would phone Miriam, see what she had to say about it.

"Who's Miriam?" she asked jealously.

"My wife. She'll understand, I'm sure."

"I might have known you had a wife." She thought, *If I'd had a father like* that …

At dinner that night, she said, "What did I do today? Why, I had lunch with Abner Zeiss."

"That man, he got a weird voice," Pompey said. "But just the same, I like that guy."

"Who is he, anyway?" John asked, pushing back his hair with a hand.

"A man with good credentials," Norma said, snickering, and when he phoned, later in the evening, hooted. "I have to laugh at you, you and Douglas," she told John. "You both think you're so great…look at Margo, racing to the telephone."

And Margo, making a face, said, "I asked him to marry me, what do you think of *that?*" and went to the phone.

"Is this the girl with the pretty flower face?" the nasal voice asked.

"It's Margo, for good or bad. Hello, Abner."

"Hello to you. I'll make you a deal. Have lunch with me and I'll have dinner with you. I'm staying at the Lion's Head Inn. I haven't seized on a place for lunch tomorrow, but I'll find some esoteric eatery, never fear. Pick me up at the hotel, okay?"

"Yes, fine."

"And I'm invited there for dinner?"

"Absolutely."

"Then about one in the lobby here."

"Yes, Abner, yes, fine."

• • •

He was buying postcards in the lobby. "I'm partial to these things," he informed her. "Taken two decades ago, I wot. Look at the clothes! And the hairdos…shades of World War II. Frances Langford and Betty Grable. Oh yes, lunch. Ah hah! I found just the place, Italian. Got your appetite with you?"

"Um hum."

It was Giovanni's, with artificial flowers and a lot of little kids belonging to the family who ran the restaurant. Running in and running out. Great, dark eyes and extravagant gestures. The canelloni was delicious, the eggplant Parmigiana worth a hand kiss. Mr. Zeiss said he'd be sorry to leave Cranford. "It's so historic," he said. "Very much to my taste. Here, have some of this bread; you can't get better in Italy."

"You're not leaving," Margo said, alarmed. "Not when I just met you!"

"Parting is such sweet sorrow," he said nasally, and the word *parting* made her think of Benjamin Brand's letters. "You must read them," she told him. "I wept a furtive tear."

"*Una furtiva lacrima,*" he said absently, and raised his voice for the bartender. "Michelob," he said boomingly. "Innkeeper, bring on the foaming froth. And any dancing girls you have handy."

"Yes, yes, Mr. Zeiss," the owner said, dashing out from behind the bar. "And how are you today, Mr. Zeiss?"

"Liverish," Abner said genially. "How's your dear wife?"

"She died last year."

"Some guys have all the luck."

"Abner," Margo chided, when the man went off for their beer.

"Therefore never send to hear for whom the bell tolls," he said. "It tolls for thee. As a matter of fact Miriam has Parkinson's Disease. But I don't wear my heart on my sleeve and neither does she."

"She has?" Margo asked, stricken.

"Yes, rather a wreck these days. Wreck or not I love her. Now what about those letters you were mentioning?"

"When we leave here, come back with me and I'll show you."

"What's for dinner tonight?"

"I don't know, but it's always something tasty."

"I'm invited, I hope?"

"I told you you were."

"Fine. I didn't sleep much last night. Can I nap a bit in some upper bedchamber?"

"Yes, mine, I'd be honored."

"Just the two of us," he said cozily. "I like the sound of that."

"You're a fraud, you wouldn't cheat Miriam, I can see it in your honest eyes."

"You may just be right."

"You're such a darling."

"So are you," he said. "So are you, my dear, and you'll make some man very happy."

"D'you think so?"

"I know so. I'd stake my life on it."

He downed three bottles of Michelob. It disappeared into the cavern of his enormous belly, which he patted comfortably, and then they walked down Main Street to Margo's car. "Oh, Mr. Zeiss," a local matron said, darting up. "How are *you* today?"

"A bit under the weather."

"But you look so well! I'm surprised you should say such a thing."

Abner reached out and clamped a firm hand on her arm. "You know the story about Noah Webster, I presume?"

"No, Mr. Zeiss." The townswoman, in her clean and starched housedress, faded from many launderings, looked up at the giant with the enormous belly. "I don't, please tell me."

"Noah Webster," Abner told his captive audience, "came home unexpectedly one day and found his wife in bed with another man. Who was the other man? I don't know, perhaps his best friend, that's the way it generally happens, isn't it? In all the operas, soap operas, bad movies and real life. However. The faithless woman looked up horrified. 'Noah, you're surprised?' she whispered.

" 'No, Madam. I'm astonished. *You're* surprised.' "

There was a brief silence. "Is that a true story?" the woman finally asked, looking befuddled.

"Apocryphal, most likely."

"You mean a President of the United States…you mean—"

"A President of the United States," Abner thundered. "A President of …" He glowered at her. "Noah Webster wrote the *Dictionary*," he said testily. "Aardvark, aardwolf, Aaronic, abaca, abacinate ..." He towered over her; for a moment she was uncertain, intimidated. Then he folded his hands across his stomach, beamed at her, told her she had hair like cornsilk, said he hoped her daughters would marry well. He picked up one of her clean, scrubbed hands and kissed it gallantly.

"Now get home to your waiting spouse," he said, and wished her a good day.

"You are not to be believed," Margo said, and he told her that, on the contrary, he was an adorable guy, and helped her into the front seat of her car. "A catnap first and then I hope a hearty dinner," he said, climbing in beside her. "Maybe steak, maybe fried chicken, perhaps pot roast, Yankee Pot Roast. My mouth is watering, just thinking about it. Boy, can that boy of yours turn a skittle."

"You only had his wheat cakes," she said. "Wait till you taste his chef d'oeuvres."

"With that saintly face of yours, no one would ever guess you could talk so dirty," he said, and she burst out laughing.

"Oh, Abner!"

"That's what I like to see," he said comfortably. "A pretty girl with a smile on her face."

...

He did nap in her bedroom, and came down, sleepy-eyed, at seven fifteen, after Pompey stood at the door, banging on it, and telling him to wake up, drinks were being served. "Mr. Abner, Mr. Abner!"

Norma said, "You're right, he is rather an old dear, listen to him snorting and snarling up there."

But he finally clattered down the stairs, drank liberally, and also downed several glasses of wine at the table. Pompey had made veal birds, with small artichokes and little shallots and roast potatoes. "For *you*, I'd consider divorcing my wife," Abner told the servant. "Just learn to make a real good matzoh-ball soup and the deal's made. We'll live happily ever after, my good man."

"Just give me the recipe and I'll make it," Pompey said, vaingloriously, the praise going to his head.

Abner Zeiss went off, after eating his way through Pompey's substantial dinner, at a little after ten. He called next morning, inviting Margo to lunch. "We seem to be going steady," she said.

"I found this fabulous place," he told her. "A little Heinie who made a cutesie little Weingarten just like in Sievering. I'll ply you with liquor and good food and then have my way with you. You didn't think my intentions were honorable, did you?"

"That's the trouble, I'm afraid they are."

"You're asking for it," he warned. "Pick me up, say one o'clock or so and I'll treat you to Wiener Schnitzel and Kartoffel Klasse. You couldn't get better in Yorkville."

• • •

It was a drive of about half an hour, then Abner grabbed her arm. "Turn here."

They bumped along a side road and came to an absolutely *unreal* garden restaurant…unreal, that was, for upstate New York with its white-clapboarded inns and gambrel-roofed houses, its Grant Wood town halls and spired churches. There was a large garden with old fruit trees and a grape arbor and waiters in Bavarian costume. Abner was right: it could have been Grinzing or Nussdorf, and two men dressed in loden sat on stools and played Viennese music.

Wienerblud, Wienerblud …

"You made this up," Margo said, as they were seated at a rude table with a red and white checked cloth. "It's simply a figment of your wild imagination."

"Of course it is," he said imperturbably. "You're dreaming, you're home in bed, dreaming."

A waiter came over, rosy-cheeked and beaming. "So, ladies and gentlemen, what will you have? I recommend the Kassler Rippchen."

"Nope. Wiener Schnitzel," Abner said. "Bring us some beer first."

"Loewenbrau?"

"And plenty of it."

Ja ja. A click of the heels and he was gone.

"When you leave, you won't forget me, will you?" Margo asked wistfully.

"Certainly not. I'll write you impassioned letters every other day."

"You won't, but I wish you would. Incidentally, you didn't seem very interested in my old family letters. You never asked to see them."

"Accidentally on purpose," he said blandly. "How can I expect to be asked to dinner every night if there isn't some excuse…like those letters I keep forgetting?"

"You don't need an excuse," she said fondly. "You're invited to dinner again tonight, and tomorrow night, and for as long as you're here."

"Oh, I'm a wily sort."

"It's so funny about rapport, Abner. I can't seem to remember a time when I didn't know you."

"Mit dem Reden kommen die Leute suzammen."

"Meaning?"

"Loosely, friendship comes with conversation. German."

'I'll buy that.'

"A laiben ahf dir."

"German?"

"No, Yiddish. It translates, 'You should live and be well.' "

The waiter came back with the beer and a basket of bread, with a saucer of sweet butter nestled in ice. Abner lathered a slab of the dark bread, handed it to her. "Taste *that*," he said, "and tell me I don't know where to find good eats." Lifting his glass of beer, he toasted her.

"Zeit gezunt!"

"Same to you," she said, and shortly thereafter the Wiener Schnitzel was set before them, delicately breaded, and the potato pancakes, and a cucumber salad. They ate like gluttons, and when Abner started mulling over what to order for dessert, Margo said, "Dessert after all that?"

"We'll have the Marillen Knoedl, it's as light as a feather," Abner said, and it was absolutely marvelous. "I wouldn't *dare* get on a scale," Margo cried, but he told her women should be zoftig, with the ugly bones hidden with good, solid flesh, and promised that he would put some beef on her.

"I almost called last night when I got back to the Lion's Head," he said. "Because the man behind the desk told me about this place; he's a displaced Austrian and we have become great friends."

"If you'd called last night I wouldn't have answered," she said, and told him about the telephone calls, and then, seeing his interest and concern, told him about falling down the stairs in the middle of the night.

"So you see," she said, "I just don't answer the phone when it rings after eleven. And my car with the bad brakes…Well, what would you think, Abner?"

He looked at her with narrowed eyes. "I haven't begun to think," he said softly. "But I will now. I certainly will now."

"It's all been very wearing."

"I can quite imagine. Do you have any ideas?"

"Some. There's a gardener, a rather brutal type. I don't know. Aside from him, I can't *imagine*. You see, when I was a child, I spent all my summers here. My father's aunt, Victoria Brand, inherited the house by direct line, and by direct line I inherited it from her. Which seems to displease someone."

"Who's that young man?" he asked without equivocation.

"You mean John? Well—"

She told him the whole story. "It would seem logical that she would have willed the house to John," she finished. "But instead, it's mine. I try to put myself in his place. Wouldn't I feel angry, thwarted, unfairly treated?"

"I know I would," he said flatly.

"And so, probably, does he."

They lingered, until almost four, welcome guests, and then got up to go. "Come again, come again," the proprietor said cordially, bowing from the waist. "*Auf wiedersehen*, have a pleasant day."

When they reached her car Abner put his arms around her. "You're a groovy kid," he said, rather huskily. "What you told me today…well, I have a feeling you need me, and in view of that I won't leave for a while. Because I have the feeling that I've come in on the second act of a melodrama. Honey, let's go driving somewhere nice, with apple blossoms falling and birds singing, and then go back to your shack. Maybe I can take a catnap on your bed again. I'm an old man, after all; I need my rest."

"You're welcome," she said, tenderly. "And now let's go driving. I'll show you some old headstones, that should interest you. Douglas took me to see them."

"Who's Douglas?"

"John's twin."

"You mean two such ethereal fellas?"

"John *ethereal?*"

"Makes me think of Gilbert and Sullivan. *Patience*. 'And everyone will say, as he walks his mystic way, what a very honorable fine young man this fine young man must be.' "

"But Doug isn't like that at all," she objected.

"I don't know about Doug, but his twin is ..." He leaned forward as they came to the old church, and the old burial ground. "Jeez, this looks interesting," he said. "Let's get out and browse. I'll make a few notes. This is the ticket, boy, is this the ticket."

• • •

She had to drag him away. "Abner, it's after six," she told him. "You wanted a nap…there won't even be time for it."

"Yes, yes," he said, scribbling on a piece of paper. "I'm coming, I'm coming."

It was after seven when they got to Brand House. John was presiding at the bar. *Ethereal?* Margo thought, and decided no, very much a man of today's time. Abner stowed away three martinis, sitting between Norma and Margo. He kissed his fingers. "Just what the doctor ordered," he said. "Gorgeous girls and potent drinks."

"May I call you Abner?" Norma asked, flashing her dimpled smile.

"What else? My name's Abner and I'm not ashamed of it. I'd hate to be Jack or Bill. I smell something nice, my guess is Virginia ham. Just don't tell those in my district, they'd defrock me. My taste buds are watering shamelessly."

They sat in the candle-lit dining room and Abner had a boarding-house reach. "Excuse me, another piece of cornbread, pass the butter, please."

At the end of the evening, when he had gone off, John said, "He's the man who came to dinner. I have a feeling he'll take up residence here and never leave."

"But he's such fun," Norma cried.

"He'll eat us out of house and home. You saw what he consumed."

"He has perfect credentials," Norma said, giggling.

"He got a crush on you, Miss Margo," Pompey said. "What Mr. Doug going to think about that?"

"Oh, shut up, Pompey, let's do the dishes."

•••

Getting ready for bed, she took the phone off the hook. Twice bit, thrice shy. *This is the way we wash our clothes, so early in the morning,* she thought, standing beside the small table with the phone that clicked the busy signal over and over and over. She went into her room and climbed into bed, dreaming that Abner Zeiss gave her a music box from Vienna, which played "The Emperor Waltz." There was a scent of verbena, or perhaps she simply imagined that. Nobody used it any more, though Aunt Vicky had.

It was simply her imagination playing tricks on her.

CHAPTER THIRTEEN

She never knew what woke her. It was the humidity, perhaps, or the fine rain that had started to fall. Or an unpleasant dream? She lay in the darkness, wondering. What was it that made her wary and wakeful?

You must get a grip on yourself, she thought, and closed her eyes again. *Think of something nice, think of Douglas, for example.* *"Un elephant, se balance, ping pong…sur un assiete faiance"…My mother sang that to me*, she thought, *my long-ago mother. Where was Mother now, in Kiev or Leningrad?* What did it matter, that in her babyhood a woman had sung fey songs to her? It didn't matter, of course, and she fell into a deep sleep, so deep that she didn't hear the approach of the intruder. She lay, powerless and a victim and the veil came across her face, and she smiled, smelling the soft scent, and kissed the fabric, thinking it was her mother's dress.

Why, Mother, you came back?

In the next moment she was clawing at the air, gasping for breath. Suffocating…and the caul was over her eyes and nose and mouth, she was without breath, the air had gone from her, and she was dying.

I'm dying, she thought, almost resigned, and then thought of the sun and life and people she loved and remembered that she was young. She started fighting, saying, inside herself, *No, I won't be a victim, there are too many victims, I'm young and strong*, and she tore at the net that cut off her breathing, struggling in the bed like a great whale. She never knew she had such strength. She heard the animal noises, and they were her own noises…her arms flailed in the air…the suffocating dark enveloped her and she writhed, pitting herself against the unseen enemy. She fought the smothering thing and conquered it, sat up in bed, filling her lungs with air, and screamed, "Where are you, where are you… show yourself!"

Someone glided out of the room, she could see the outline of a figure, unclearly, in the misty moonlight, a wraith of a shadow sliding out and through the door. Breathing deep, a hand on her chest, she gathered herself together and sprang up, coughing. She reeled across the room, found the door, fumbling, threw it open. Wheezing, frantic, she stumbled out into the corridor.

It was empty, there was no one there. The wall sconces, softly lit against the darkness of the night, that was all, and the pale light of the moon through the windows at both ends. Otherwise it was silent and deserted.

She screamed.

No one came.

She screamed again.

A voice, belated enough, called down. "What's that?"

It was John's voice.

She screamed again, and this time kept on screaming. Things blurred around her, but she finally saw John, in a maroon-colored robe.

"What the hell goes on here?" he demanded, and she saw him, wavering and indistinct, and screamed again.

"Margo," he said sharply, his voice cutting the quiet like a knife. "Margo…what happened?"

"They tried to kill me," she screamed.

"*What?*"

"Came into my room, tried to smother me …"

The hand that slammed across her face brought water into her eyes, sent her reeling. But it did the trick: she stopped screaming, and things began to focus again. They were there, in the dimly-lit corridor, she and John, and her wits came back to her. He put a hand on her shoulder.

"Tell me," he said, quietly.

"Someone came into my room," she said just as quietly. "Someone tried to smother me."

"Was it a dream?" he asked.

"Damn you," she said without emphasis. "Damn you, will you listen?"

"I'm listening," he said. "I'm listening. Talk."

"I woke up and someone was trying to smother me."

"How?"

"With a caul."

"What's a caul?"

"Babies are born with it. Some babies are born with it."

"Were you?"

"I don't know how I was born, I was just born, that's as much as I know."

"What made you think of a caul?"

"It was like that. Like the fishing nets I've seen in Italy, in France. Coming over my face. I'll have to go away. They want me dead here."

Home, she thought, and felt the weak tears surfacing. Home? Where in God's name was home? She had no home. Except for this house; only someone didn't want her here.

"Who would want harm to come to you?" John asked, staring at her.

She laughed at him, at his obtuseness. "You can ask that?" she cried. "I was almost killed when my car went out of control. I fell downstairs in the middle of the night because someone was calling to me? And just now someone came into my room and tried to suffocate me? Imagination, is that what you think? And the telephone ringing night after night?"

He had his hands in the pockets of his robe. "Pompey did tell me about the telephone," he said. "But I—"

"Night after night. I started taking the receiver off the hook. Imagination, you say? And then this caul over my face? Are you trying to tell me I'm insane?"

"I didn't say that."

"The way you're looking at me! Maybe it was you, maybe it was Ben, I told Norma I'd throw him off the place. Maybe it was—"

"Margo, you're not making sense."

"If someone did these things to you, you wouldn't make sense either," she cried. "You *honorable* young man; what a very, very honorable, fine young man this fine young man must be. Oh, get away from me, get away. I want Pompey, Pompey…I want Pompey!"

And suddenly Pompey was there, holding her, and then putting her to bed, bending over her in the soft light of the lamp he had lit. "Tell me," he said. "Tell me, Miss Margo."

"Why, someone here wants me dead," she said flatly.

Rocking her back and forth in his arms, he crooned, "Don't think them things, they're not true, how can they be true?"

"Don't give me that," she said. "I'm in danger, don't you realize that?"

"Miss Margo—"

"I'm putting you on notice. When I'm dead you just remember that I told you. You just remember, Pompey."

She saw John standing in the doorway and sat up. "You too," she said. "You remember too. And when I end up on a stone slab, you think of what I said tonight. And then see if you can sleep, either. You'll see, you'll see—"

"It's all right, Mr. John," Pompey said. "Go back to sleep. I'll take care of her, don't worry."

• • •

She slept, woke, looked up. "Pompey, are you there?"

"Yes, darling."

"You won't go away."

"I won't go away."

The tree frogs sang, the night turned into a pale dawn. "Pompey, are you there?" the anxious voice asked.

"Yes, Miss Margo."

"I'm all right now. Don't leave me. Wait until I brush my teeth, okay? I'll come down with you. Could you make me some griddle cakes? But don't leave until I'm ready, you promise?"

"I promise."

"Thanks for staying with me. I'm not crazy, I know I'm not crazy. Someone was in this room, and they put the caul over my face, and wanted me dead."

"But Miss Margo, who would want that?"

"I don't know. Someone does. You ask me why? I don't know. All I know is that it happened, and I'll never forget it, not to my dying day. Hate is a horrible thing; someone hates me. I don't know why, I just don't know why,"

• • •

There were two eggs, sunny-side up, toast with butter, charred bacon, and the sun streamed into the cheerful dining room. It seemed light years away now, that someone had come into her bedroom, put a shroud around her face, and maliciously tried to do evil to her. John came down, dressed for work, troubled, questioning. "You'll be all right?" he asked.

"Yes, John. Thanks."

"I'll be home early this evening."

"Thanks very much."

He went off, his car chugging down the drive.

An hour later, while she slowly dressed, there was a telephone call from Abner Zeiss. He was querulous. "Pompey said you'd been attacked in the night," he said. "What happened, for Christ's sweet sake?"

"Someone in my room, trying to smother me."

"Who?"

"If I knew I'd be happy to say," she answered, and there was a thoughtful silence.

"I said a melodrama, didn't I?" he reminded her.

"You weren't far off."

"Sweetheart, get dressed and meet me in Mithford at noon. Get out of that house. There's a small town called Harper's Crossing, just outside of Picksville. Ask Pompey, he'll tell you how to get there."

"Yes, Abner, thanks, thanks very much."

She was just so grateful. She thought of presents to take him, and raked through her possessions, finding a book a French savant had given her—*The Life and Times of the Wandering Jew*, one of the most fascinating books she had ever read—and a book of short stories by a 19th-century author, Franz Gottschalk, one of her treasures, discovered in a small bookshop in Marseilles. And at the last moment she stuffed Benjamin Brand's letters into a manila envelope.

Armed with these small gifts, all she had to offer, she drove off to the small town of Mithford, three quarters of an hour away, putting aside all worries and sorrows, and at just before twelve noon found the place Abner had described. It was another outdoor restaurant, but this time very Colonial, at the back of a house she gauged to be 18th-century, perhaps at one time a manor house much like Brand House. There was a flagpole, where the standard flapped in a smart breeze, furling and unfurling the Stars and Stripes, and the tables were laid with pristine damask cloths, the menus purple-inked, with the average entree seven dollars or more.

Abner sat, all two hundred pounds of him, having a palaver with the owner. As she approached the table she heard him saying, "Did you know, sir, that where this restaurant is, Walt Whitman started his immortal poem cycle, 'Leaves Of Grass'?"

She stood there, unseen and listening, while Abner proclaimed, his beard quivering and his eyes alight.

> *"On my way a moment I pause*
> *Here for you! And here for America!*
> *Still, the present I raise aloft,*
> *Still the future of the States,*
> *I harbinger glad and sublime,*
> *And for the past I pronounce*
> *What the air holds of the red Aborigines ..."*

"That's very nice," the proprietor said politely.

"Nice? It's immortal," Abner snorted, and then saw Margo. "Come forward, lass," he cried. "Why dost thou hidst thyself?" She sat down across from him and he groped for her hand. In his nasal voice, his red mouth half-hidden by his beard, he proclaimed, "So some old vagabond, in mud who grovels/ Dreams, nose in air, of Edens sweet to roam/ Wherever smoky wicks illumine hovels/ He sees another Capua or Rome."

"Hello, Abner," Margo said.

"Hello, my pretty. This is a steak place; how do you want it, rare, medium rare or well done?"

"Medium rare."

"Two medium rare," he told the proprietor. "But first, ale, a bottle each."

"Coming up," the proprietor said, and disappeared. "It's nice, isn't it?" Abner commented, and she said yes, it was lovely, every lunch she had had with him was lovely. "I brought you some things to please you," she told him. "I have to reciprocate somehow."

He looked at the books, exclaimed over them, and then opened the packet of letters. "Benjamin Brand," he said. "Shades of Melville."

"Benjamin? As I remember, it was Ishmael."

"Same period, same names," he said, and started reading the letters. "Very sentimental," he commented, and the ale was brought, but he didn't touch the bottle. He seemed, instead, to be intent on Benjamin Brand's letters to his lady. She was just as glad of the hiatus, glancing around with pleasure at the environs, the outlying gardens and the American flag waving in the breeze, and the smell of thousands of flowers.

So that she was startled when he said, "Jesus, would you believe it!" She turned to him, questioning.

"What, Abner?"

His eyes were brilliant. "But darling," he said. "This last letter, for sake. It has a stamp from Mauritius, an island in the Indian Ocean, one of the Mascarene Islands. Why, you babe in the wood, it's a collector's item, any philatelist would be happy to fork over thousands of dollars for it! Maybe—"

"For the stamp?" she asked, incredulous.

"Don't you know *anything* about stamps?" he demanded.

"It wasn't ever part of my curriculum at school," she said tartly. "You mean the stamp has value?"

"Take my word for it, it has value, dollar value."

"How interesting," she said. "I have ten more of the same."

His eyes seemed to hang out of his head. "What do you mean, ten more of the same?" he asked, his voice ragged.

"The crew wrote letters at the same time. The same stamps. Ten of them. Noah, Ezekiel, Luke...*you* know, the way they used to be named. It was so heartwarming, their letters...Abner, let go of my arm!"

"But he said. Margo, don't you *realize?*"

"Realize what?" she asked, but a little thrill ran through her. "Realize what, Abner?"

"Ten more of the same *ten more* ..." He became incoherent. my child, if you have eleven of these stamps...eleven ..."

"Well, yes," she said, still chilled with an unknown knowledge. "This last letter and ten more. That makes eleven, if I'm not mistaken. I was always rather poor at arithmetic."

He looked at her for a long time. Then said, "Eleven of these stamps? My dear child, all told, they are worth about sixty thousand dollars. These are the first stamps issued by a British Colonial outpost, and to boot, they were printed hastily, and wrong. Instead of saying 'Post paid' they said 'Post Office.' Any stamp collector would give his arm or leg or whatever. If, as you say, you have ten more of these stamps, you're a rich woman... can't I get that through your head?"

"And she knew that?"

There was a fractional silence. Then hairy Abner said, "Who knew what?"

"My aunt. I was told she had left me a fortune."

"Who told you that?"

"A woman in these parts, a friend of my aunt's."

"That could be," Abner said. "Yes, your aunt must have known what these stamps meant in cash value. You're richer today than you were yesterday. How does that strike you, my child?"

"I don't know," she said.

"But you should be happy, deliriously happy."

"I would be," she said, "if she were alive. She meant so much to me, and now she's dead. Everything else seems so paltry."

"Ah so," Abner said, and looked over at her with comprehension in his eyes. "Just the same, she's dead, that woman you loved, and she left you this. Why don't you just be glad for it, and know it was what she wanted?"

"Yes, she must have known," Margo agreed. "I'm sure she must have known. The palindrome."

"The palindrome?"

"I didn't tell you about that. She left a message for me, a palindrome."

Her thoughts drifted to a telephone conversation, *"You're to be here tomorrow."*

"I can't, Auntie."

"But then, as soon as possible …"

Strong, vibrant voice. And the death. "What are you thinking?" Abner asked.

"That she was…that she didn't die a natural death."

"What makes you so certain?"

"I'm not certain. Yes, I am certain. Yes. Now I'm certain. Someone killed her."

"Better have proof," he said. "Better have proof." He leaned across the table, filling her wine glass. "Drink up," he said. "Drink up, *Bubeleh* …"

They ate and drank. "We're Adam and Eve," Abner said, "a man and a woman. The first man and the first woman. I'm Adam and you're Eve. Happy to make your acquaintance, Eve. What the hell did you do with my rib? I have a sharp pain."

"Adam," Margo said slowly. "Adam."

"The first man," Abner said, lighting a cigar.

"Yes, yes. But Adam! The Adam desk! Ed Corliss found the letters in the Adam desk…the desk in the Long Room, he said. Well, the desk in the Long Room is an Adam desk. I told you about the palindrome…she knew she was in danger, and she wrote that message to me—MADAM, I'M ADAM—and gave me a clue. Abner, you must realize now—I realize now—she knew something was going to happen, and she wanted me to have security…those letters…"

He thought about it. Finally looked up at her. "Yes," he said. "You could be right. That she was afraid, and wanted to secure your future. The palindrome? That's very revealing. She must have …"

"She must have been threatened," Margo said.

"It seems logical enough," he admitted.

"More than logical," she said coldly. "She sensed what was in store for her and took steps."

"As if I were there I can see it," she said, talking rapidly. "She knew what she knew…and apparently she loved me, as Clara—Pompey's sister—said. I was her blood, and she wanted me to inherit, and made out her will that way. But there was a malignant presence, and she knew that, so she wrote me that code thing, the palindrome, and Ed Corliss found the letters in the Adam desk, and now, according to you, I'm richer by sixty thousand dollars, maybe more. And that being the case, what will they do now?"

"Who's they?" Abner asked. "Who stands to gain by your not being there?"

"John," she said promptly.

"Why?"

"Because he's lived there from boyhood on. If not for me, he'd stay there, be curator."

"Oh?"

"Yes, can't you see that?"

He thought about it. "Yes," he finally said. "I do see it." He narrowed his eyes. "You may have guessed the truth, that she was afraid, that she knew something was in the wind. You say, John, without hesitation. Are you sure you've given this enough thought?"

John…a hand dashing dark hair back. Long lean legs crossed indolently. Until she came home from her wanderings, John had every right to expect that he would be lord of the manor. She did *not* suspect Douglas. Any fool could see that Douglas was madly in love with his acres. So if not Doug, then John…who else?

"Drink up," Abner said. "Get some alcohol down your gullet, you need it. And if I seem absent minded it's only because I'm doing some thinking. Yes, and let them know, tonight, about the stamps. I want them to know. I won't be there for dinner tonight, I'll be an absentee. Yes, I mean that. Because I want them to hear about the windfall that's come your way. If you have eleven stamps of the Mauritius vintage 1847, as you assure me you have, then you are richer by, say sixty thousand dollars, than you were yesterday. Let them know that; it may make all the difference. And Margo—"

"Yes, Abner?"

"Call me at any hour, even if it's four in the morning," he said. "Don't hesitate. I'll be there, if you need me, and I want you to remember that."

"Yes, Abner."

"Just don't forget it," he said, and got up. "You drive me home now," he said. "And remember what I said."

"You're not coming to dinner tonight?"

"Not tonight," he said. "For reasons known only to myself. You just tell them about the stamps, and we'll take it from there. And Margo—"

"Yes, what?"

"Be careful."

"I've learned to be," she said. "I thought I'd made it clear."

"Then be *more* careful," he said, and they drove back to Cranford, where she dropped him off at the Lion's Head Inn, and then went on home. The thrill of fear was very much like the thrill of pleasure…engaging the nerve ends, and tickling the scalp. Afraid? Yes…very. Forewarned, however, was forearmed. *I won't be caught napping again*, she thought, and informed them at dinner.

"Letters with valuable stamps, collector's items," she said, watching their faces. "Abner Zeiss thinks about sixty thousand, nothing to be sneezed at, you must agree. It means I can keep this house, live here."

"In the sticks?" Norma asked incredulously.

"I'm fond of this part of the country."

John looked up. "So after all, you won't leave," he said.

"I can't quite believe it, but there you are."

Pompey went downstairs, to the cellar, and brought up a bottle of Mumm's. Wiping off the cobwebs, he put it between his knees and popped the cork. "She saved this and some others for your wedding," he told Margo. "However, this is as good an occasion as any."

They drank, clinking glasses. "To you," Norma cried, lifting her glass. "To you, Margo, you always were the winner."

And she watched their faces, but there was no face that gave itself away. There was only laughter, congenial laughter, and nothing to raise her suspicions. When Abner called, at just after nine, she confessed that it had all been very pleasant and nothing to tell other than that.

"Maybe it's only my imagination too," he said.

"Maybe," she agreed, half willing to settle for that.

"Meet me for lunch tomorrow in Comstock," he said. "Pompey will give you directions."

"About one?"

"More or less."

• • •

It was New England at its best, a Greek Revival house, run down in these days, but once as splendid as could be; it was simply that times had changed and the 20th century taken over the 19th. The room in which they dined on lake trout and buttery asparagus had once seen ladies and gentlemen sipping claret and flirting, lovely faces hiding behind feathered fans and men in morning coats, bowing from the waist.

"*Sic transit,*" Abner said in his Bronx accent.

"Yes, indeed," Margo answered.

"So you told them about your good fortune," he said.

"Yes, they said very best wishes and that seemed to be that."

"No peculiar expressions?"

"None whatever."

"That's rather hard lines," he said. "After all, we have to prepare for the third and final act."

"As dramatic as that?"

"I have this feeling that, yes, it's as dramatic as that."

She palmed a chin in her hand. "You'll form some ideas, possibly. At dinner. You have insight I don't claim to possess. You may see what I failed to see."

"Not tonight," he said. "There's a little library in Roundsville I've been told about. I'll stay the weekend there. Tell Pompey I'll eat like a pig on Monday."

"You're deserting me?"

"Only for the weekend. Nothing ever happens on weekends. Brownstones are robbed from Monday to Friday, but on the weekends never. You'll be all right for the nonce …"

He lifted his arm, and the waiter came over. "A repeat on the apple pie," he said. "Mother never made it better."

They walked through country gardens later. Flower beds with heliotrope borders, century-old elms with their branches reaching into the sky, the spire of a local church spiking into the blue. *Europe is lovely*, Margo thought, *but so is America*, and she remembered what she had sung in Assembly many, many years ago.

> "O beautiful for spacious skies
>   For amber waves of grain,

For purple mountain majesties
Above the fruited plain.
America, America, God shed his grace on thee,
And crown thy good with brotherhood
From sea to shining sea."

CHAPTER FOURTEEN

It was a quiet dinner hour. Norma was absent. "Working over-time," John said.

They drank their martinis, almost silent, later picked at their dinner. Pompey said, "What's the problem, you don't like flank steak?"

"It's fine, just that I'm fagged out," Margo said.

"This fresh asparagrass cost an arm and a leg, how come you let it get cold? Everything going to waste."

The candles flickered.

Later, in the Long Room, John said, "Let's go to the Tap Room for drinks, Margo."

"It's too late," she objected.

"It's just after nine," he pointed out.

"But I'm tired. You must be too."

There was a long, uneasy silence. Then he said, "Very well, Margo, I get the message. No need to say more." She started to protest, but he left the room, erect and stiff, and a few minutes later she heard the sound of his car zooming down the driveway. Pompey came in, collecting glasses and overflowing ashtrays from the cocktail hour. "Mr. John go out?" he asked. "Seems I heard his car."

"He wanted drinks at the Tap Room."

"Why didn't you go with him?"

"Because I didn't want to."

"If it was Mr. Douglas, you'd go, ain't that so?"

"All right, Pompey, let it go."

He grinned. "Just the same, it would be different if it was Mr. Douglas."

"Maybe. But it wasn't. I'm going to bed."

"You just do that. I'll make you a nice breakfast, some of the left-over steak, and jumbo eggs, corn fritters, probably. Come on, give Pompey a kiss and then scoot up."

She pressed her lips to his weathered cheek.

"That's my girl," he said. "Now you get on up. You got shadows under your pretty eyes."

"Have I?"

"You miss her, don't you?"

"Yes, Pompey, I miss her."

"Me too."

She watched him, as she climbed the stairs, coming and going in his duties. A lifetime spent in service. *They also serve who only stand and wait*, she thought, and in her room brushed her hair, looked about, knowing that everything in this house belonged to her. A charmed life …

Who could have dreamed that a few letters, with foreign stamps, would make the difference between what you wanted but couldn't have, and what you wanted and *could* have?

The telephone, ringing, sent her to the instrument.

"It's me, Norma."

"Oh, hello, darling. I missed you tonight."

"I missed you too."

"John said you were working overtime."

"Did he?" She laughed, a silvery sound. "Not at all. I'm home and alone. He and I had a little difference of opinion. I don't go along with some of his ideas and vice versa."

"Oh, well …"

"Look, pet, I'm feeling a bit low. Can I ask this of you? Come to see me? I'd love to have you here for a drink. Is it wanting too much?"

"What happened between you and John, Norma?"

"Sometimes I hate him. Forget I said that. Just…can you pop over for a drink? It's not very late."

Her good luck…and Norma's malaise. "Of course," she said. "Of course, Norma. I'll leave right now."

"I don't like to ask for favors, but I'm really rather blue."

"I'll get into my car straightaway."

"I knew I could depend on you," Norma said. "I knew it. I just knew it."

…

Norma's flat was one flight up a steep staircase. The apartment was very attractive, cheerful and lamp-lit. Norma met her at the door. "Thanks for answering my Mayday call," she said. "I've built a pitcher of martinis."

"*That* sounds good. Norma, this place is lovely."

"It doesn't cost very much, and of course I added my own touches."

She pointed out the built-in cabinets and bookcases. "I designed them," she said. "And Ben Blough did the work. I do think they came out rather well."

"Why, it's fantastic; you're a wizard, Norma."

"I have taste, if that's what you mean. Not much else, but I do have taste."

"And a lot more besides. Don't be silly."

"Well, sit down."

She filled glasses. "As good as John's?" she asked.

"The martinis? Just as good, perhaps better."

"So you see, he isn't the be-all and end-all."

Norma sat down. "You see, Margo, John and I don't always see eye to eye. And so, this afternoon, we had a little argument. He left the office, not saying, 'Dinner as usual, my sweet,' and so I came home and fixed some red snapper for myself, but suddenly I couldn't bear to be alone any longer. Forgive me, Margo, but thanks, many thanks for coming to see me."

"Why, I'm so happy to see where you live."

"Then you like it?"

"It's really charming."

"Nothing much compared to Brand House."

"But it's so…comfy Norma, and in the best of taste. I'm sure you're very happy here."

"I've known worse," Norma said. "Do you want to play cards?"

"No, let's just talk."

"Yes, I'd prefer that too. Another drink?"

"They're stronger than Pompey's…well, maybe another *half* one."

But Norma filled her glass to the brim. The liquor *did* go to her head, Margo thought, trying to clear it, and although there was a cross current of breezes in Norma's flat, she felt rather uncomfortably warm. "Yes," Norma said. "It's a very hot night, Margo. How about going for a swim?"

"At this hour? And anyway, I don't have a suit."

"I have dozens of them. A new one too; I've never worn it."

"But it's really getting quite late, isn't it?"

"You don't have to get up in the morning," Norma said. "I do, but it doesn't matter."

"Well—"

"I just have a craving to drive out to the lake and take a dip. Just the two of us against the world. By that I mean men, of course. I can't tell you how much they upset me at times. You too, I'm sure. We're women in a man's world. But if you're tired—"

"No, it isn't that. No, and I don't mind at all. It would be rather fun, I guess."

"Well, you *are* a darling. Come on in the bedroom, there's a suit, as I said, I've never worn, it still has the tags on it. I bought it in Ottawa, where I went for my vacation this year. It'll fit; we're the same size."

She dragged it out of a closet. It was very pretty, sea-green, brief and low in the back. Margo pulled up the straps, and walked into the living room. "How do I look?"

"Like a mermaid. Well, that is a stunning suit. What did John say about your coming here tonight?"

"John? I didn't see him. He went off, in his car, to the Tap Room of the hotel."

"And Pompey?"

"Why, in bed before I left. He has a long day's work; he goes to bed with the chickens."

"Poor soul. All right, shall we go, then? It won't take me a minute to change into a bathing suit. Be out in two shakes of a lamb's tail. Finish your drink while waiting."

But the drink was too strong. On an impulse, Margo upturned it into a plant on a window sill. She had had quite enough, and longed for the fresh air to clear her head. Thankfully, Norma didn't take too long. She came out in a crimson-red tank suit, showing off her lovely figure to full advantage. "It may be cool," she said. "I see you brought a sweater, and I'm taking along this mohair shawl."

"How lovely, it looks like gossamer," Margo said, and Norma told her it had been bought on her vacation in Canada.

"We'll go in your car," Norma said, "then you can drop me off afterwards, and I promise you it won't be late. I have to get my beauty sleep. But it's a divine night, isn't it?"

It was. Warm and mellow, and the cicadas sang, a bullfrog in some lily pond harrumphed hoarsely. Cities seemed very far away, the night was a country night, the moon was a country moon. *I do feel I belong here*, Margo thought, as they climbed into her car, and now she had come into a fortune, would probably live here. She was almost certain that her aunt had known about the stamps, that she had meant them as insurance…and again the uneasy feeling.

Why hadn't she lived to tell about them? That strong voice… "*I shall expect you tomorrow …*"

Norma's shawl billowed out. Pale aqua, soft and scented, wrapped around the slender shoulders. "Oh, sorry," Norma said, and gathered it around her again. For a moment there was a feeling of having seen that shawl before, soft and enveloping and lightly scented …

As if she had worn it herself, or had it wrapped around her. "What is it?" Norma asked, her great, jewel eyes looking sideways.

"Nothing. Remember when we used to say, 'Last one to the raft's a rotten egg?'"

"I remember everything," Norma said. "That's the way I am. It sticks with me. Yes, I remember, Margo. Things even you may have forgotten."

"I have a pretty good recall," Margo commented, and drove ahead, under the orange-colored moon, and the smells of the summer night in her nostrils. She thought, I *love country roads at night, just the headlamps of the car and that great, dark distance ahead.* There was a fragrance to a country night that was more potent than the most expensive perfume. And almost contiguous to her thoughts, Norma asked abruptly, "What's that perfume you're wearing?"

"I'm not sure. I just dabbed something on before dinner."

"It's heady. Forty dollars an ounce, if I'm not mistaken."

"I don't know."

"It smells the way it should if you can afford to pay forty dollars an ounce for it."

It was a little distasteful, Margo thought, the emphasis on money. And for the first time she thought, *This girl might have learned many things, but underneath there's a certain vulgarity.*

And then she scolded herself. Norma had pulled herself up by her bootstraps. No one to help or guide her. And she had, in the main, done very well. Her voice was nicely modulated, her skin clear, eyes bright, and her manner almost without fault.

Don't judge, she told herself, and saw the sign up ahead.

Lake Aladdin.

Always, she had loved the name for the lake. Not one of those American Indian names that abounded in these parts…Lake Minnewaska, Lake Amantaska …

Her lake had a more romantic sound.

"How come they named it that?" she asked, as she parked the car.

"Named it what?"

"I mean the lake. Lake Aladdin."

Norma sat quietly.

"It's such a pretty, unexpected name. I always wondered about it."

"I didn't," Norma said, and opened the door on her side. "Shall we go?"

"Yes, let's."

Both doors banged shut. They stood on the brow of the woody hill that led down to the water. Margo looked up. "Hot day tomorrow," she said. "Moon's red as fire."

"Like a watermelon."

"Oh, I wish you hadn't said that. Suddenly I yearn for a slice of watermelon."

"Remember when we used to bury our faces in it?"

"Yes, and plant the seeds in the earth. We were always so sure we'd have our own watermelon garden."

"But nothing ever happened," Norma said. "That's the way of things."

The shawl flew in Margo's face again. This time it nettled her, displeased her. She pushed it back, away from her. There was that faint, strangely familiar scent again. Like musk, like —

"Well, let's make our way down and wet our feet," Norma said, and threw the shawl off, folding it in her hands. They clambered down the woodsy trail and then stood at the edge of the water. Margo dropped her sweater and looked at Norma, who stood, straight as an arrow, her lovely body perfect in every detail, an Aphrodite. "All right, let's take the plunge," she said, and walked into the water.

Margo followed, in a kind of transport. The water was cold, almost as cold as ice, and bracing, and wonderful. She threw back her head. "And to think I won't ever go away," she said. "Imagine it, I won't ever go away."

"You're going to stay, then?"

"Yes, yes."

"And live in that house?"

"Why yes, of course. I'm able to now."

A night bird, perhaps an owl, or even, God forbid, a bat, flew across their faces. "Uhg," Margo cried, and splashed shoulder deep into the water. "What was that?"

"I think a gull," Norma said. "They come here because people fish. I've heard they've wounded several persons. They go for the eyes."

"My God …"

"They're not as nice as they look, all silver and pretty. Lots of things aren't as nice as they look." She put an arm around Margo's shoulder. "So you're going to stay, after all."

"Apparently." She heard her own deep-throated laugh, a laugh of pure joy and wonderment, and then stood tense. There was a quick glimpse, and an expression in the eyes, and the quiet, intent posture. Yes. And something she had tried to pin down a few nights ago came to her.

Something from the long ago.

Two small girls and two boys five or six years older:

Doug: "Margo's the fairest of them all. Mirror mirror on the wall, Margo's the fairest of them all."

And John: "That's not very nice, Doug."

"Oh, can it, you dog."

"Don't call me a dog."

"Margo's the fairest of them all," Doug chanted again. "Mirror, mirror on the wall ..."

John: "It isn't polite; Norma's pretty too"

"Not at all, she's just fair to middling."

"That's a kind of rotten thing to say."

A fist fight.

Margo: "Let's leave them. Come on, Norma, they're not being... they're not being ..."

"Not being nice? They're just saying the truth. You are prettier than I am. I'm nothing, nothing."

The dark-haired girl, racked with sobs, plunging into the water. Margo following. "Please...don't listen to them, Norma ..."

"It's because of you...why don't you go away!"

"Norma, don't do that...don't...don't ..." Ducking, wheeling, she backed away. "Norma, you don't know what you're doing ..."

But the branch had come down over her head, and the waters closed around her, gushing into her eyes and nose and throat. And later, in bed, the realization...Norma had tried to hurt her. Aunt Vicky had fed her soup and toast fingers. "Forget it," she said, commandingly. "Never think of it again."

And she hadn't.

But it had been stored in her brain cells, and was alive again tonight. There was that beautiful, implacable face, the strange, intent, determined look on the lovely face of Norma Calvet.

She suddenly knew. History was repeating itself. On this humid night in mid-summer, history was repeating itself. Once again Norma Calvet wanted her, Margo, to disappear, to go out of her life, out of the lives of all of them. And her uplifted arm, holding a heavy pine branch, underwrote her deadly intention.

But ...

They were no longer children. Women, both of them, and as the past came surging back, the adrenalin flooded through Margo's veins. *Now I know,* she told herself, *now I know.* And she threw herself down in the water, plunging beneath the surface. Behind her, the branch was lowered with a harsh swish, whistling in the dark. It hit the water, making a great splash.

It was a silent battle, eerie and ghostly. When she had to surface, she saw that Norma was only yards away from her. The grim, determined face was not beautiful now, but hard and stern and almost ugly. There was a triumphant gasp and then the branch smashed down again, sending spray into Margo's eyes as it hit the water.

And again Margo plunged, swooping down once more. It was her heart, thudding wildly, that frightened her. She hadn't been able to take a deep enough breath...this time she had to surface before she had swum very far. She came up, drew air into her lungs, and saw, with horror, that Norma was only a foot or so away.

It was no longer a silent struggle. Norma, in her triumph, raised the branch, her arm arcing, power behind those young muscles. "Come and take your medicine," she cried, her voice rising hysterically. "You come here and change all our lives...I hate you, I've always hated you ..."

"You must be crazy," Margo shouted. "What do you think you're doing? If you harm me, they'll know...what do you hope to accomplish? They'll know it was you...I didn't think you were that stupid!"

"No, they won't know it was me," Norma said contemptuously. "They'll think you came here for a swim and...damn it, Margo, you were never at your shining best in the water. All of us, we grew up here, water rats. Many's the time you had to be carried ashore out of breath …"

"That was because you tried to drown me…oh, yes, I remember now!"

The branch hit the water again, this time so near Margo that she stumbled backwards, and the water swirled around her, not help but hindrance. And now she knew, irrevocably. Norma had made certain that John didn't know of her whereabouts, that Pompey didn't know…and those drinks had been potent…*too* potent. Yes, and try now as she would, she couldn't recall Norma sipping her own drink.

Then the madness of it brought some of her reason back. It was not possible that Norma meant to do this. People did all sorts of shabby things, but not casual murder: Norma was only trying to scare her away, show her she wasn't wanted here. The girl knew her family was rich…then let the rich girl leave the premises and leave it to those who belonged there.

"Norma, let's go back," she said, angered at the trembling of her voice, angered and fighting for control.

"Go back? Only one of us will go back," Norma said. "I haven't gone this far for nothing."

And now the meaning of the shawl, in a blinding insight, came to her. Like a caul…the soft, Shetland strands cast over her face… Norma's shawl, smothering her …

"It was you," she said, stunned. "It was you, in my room that night. With that shawl…you tried to—"

"Prove it," Norma said viciously. "Prove it."

"But why, but *why?*"

"Because you came here *again*. Wasn't it enough all those years ago? And now you came here again. You dare ask me *why?* Everything for you and nothing for me. You don't think I'll take that lying down?"

"What…in what way does it affect you?"

There was a cry of jubilation. Norma, rising in the lake like Venus from the sea, was suddenly beside her. "There you are," she shrieked, and the inexorable arm was raised. Margo ducked, feinted, but the branch came down across the base of her skull, sending her into a tailspin, with stars and stripes and colored circles whirling, whirling, whirling …

"Ugh," she said thickly, and then the water into which she was plunged pulled her back, a little back, the cold of it reviving her, enough so that she started struggling, weakly, flailing her arms about, and heard her own hoarse voice.

And another hoarse voice, rapid and impassioned, wild and infuriated. "Affect me! *Affect* me! Where am I going to live? Brand House is mine! If it weren't for you it would be mine! It—"

Water trickling from her mouth, her nose streaming. Breathing like an engine. Voice weak, strained. "If it weren't for me," Margo said, wheezing, "it would belong to the Historical Society."

"No! If it weren't for you she would have left it to John, it belongs to *John*. How could she *dare* leave it to you…and then, as if that weren't enough, you find something that was there all the time, and we never knew it at all. Sixty thousand dollars…those damned, rotten stamps that were there all the time, just waiting for you, for *you*." There was a kind of sob. "It's just too much to be believed, the way everything falls into your lap."

She was crying now, tears were streaming down her face. "Some people don't deserve to live," she said, raggedly.

"Norma, but Norma…if you do anything to me, how do you expect to get back? How are you going to get home again?"

"A friend is coming for me," Norma said, dashing a hand across her eyes. "A friend. And if I need help, he'll help. You're trapped, Margo. Ambushed. Your luck has run out."

"A friend…what friend?"

"Never you mind."

John.

It was the last punishment. Whatever else she might have thought about John, she could never have imagined this. John, her aunt's protege. John…

There was something evil about this upstate country, with its hexes, its inbreeding, and its burned witches all those years ago, its crooked crosses atop barns, and a girl with a beautiful face who had a stone for a heart …

Then, as if at a signal, there was the sound of a car in the night, the revving motor, and then the dying of it. "All right," Norma said, her voice sounding tired now. "Now he's here, now I'm not alone. Ben's here and you can forget about going home again. He'll come and help me. Better say a prayer, Margo, you're going to die."

"Ben?" Margo repeated, wonderingly. "Ben?"

"Of course Ben," Norma said quietly. "Of course Ben. Ben would die for me; I'm surprised you didn't catch on to that."

"You mean not John?"

There was a contemptuous laugh. "John? John, for Christ's sake. John wouldn't have the guts to—" She was babbling now, her words running into each other. "You, Margo, *you*. Coming here and wanting to take everything away from me. I knew right away that I'd have to get rid of you, and when you found those damned, infernal stamps…all that money…why, you're a witch, you should be binned on the Common, everything going your way all your life. You never did an honest day's work …"

With heroic strength Margo tried to beat off the hands that held her head under the lake water. She gasped, couldn't see, struggled wildly, felt flesh against her hands, beat against that flesh, using her nails.

"Forget it," Norma said, her voice thin and spent. "You're going to die, you've got to die. He was like a son, John was like a son. Where were you? I sat there, hour after hour, holding that horrible old hand. Where were you? We earned it, we earned it! Where were you? It's our future…you think I want to be a secretary all my life? He'll stay there, and I with him…and you'll be dead. Who are you, Golden Princess? Spoiled, rotten spoiled…we've put it off year after year…that terrible old woman…she hated me, did you know that? I wasn't good enough for her. And meanwhile, where were you? I heard about you, wonderful Margo, until it came out of my ears, and nose and throat, and gut. And you come here and want to take it all away. Die, you parasite, *die* …"

The branch came down again, like Aaron's rod. The water broke its impetus, but it was just about enough; it sent her reeling, almost senseless, into the beautiful rippling lake, and the moon was like a golden eye. Choking, sinking, she implored, "Let me live." But the water drowned her, drowned out her words, and the hands held her face under.

"I'll take over," a voice said, from somewhere very far away, and it was Ben Blough's voice, quiet and deadly. "I'll finish her off."

"No, me," the hysterical voice cried. "Let me do it, I want her to suffer, I *insist* on doing it…get away you fool, I want to—"

How could it be, Margo thought, floundering, knowing she was half dead, knowing it was the end, and tired unto death. Yet… how could it be that she heard Doug's voice?

And then other voices, muttered oaths, someone running, crashing through trees, cursing, shouting …

Bedlam …

Bedlam…crawling like some prehistoric monster, sea-creature, she heard the shouts and the cries, the quiet night no longer quiet…horror, unimaginable horror …

And then the sound of bone against bone, a sickening thing, and another curse and then once more the thud of a blow …

And the eerie, long-drawn sigh of a man in agony …

"Out like a light," Douglas said, from somewhere far away, and there was nothing else, just blackness. *Dead, I'm dead*, Margo thought, and then thought nothing more.

•••

She opened her eyes, on dry land, to the blinding light of the moon. Retching, she heard Pompey's voice. "Get that damned water out of her. Get it out, get it out …"

A scream sounded through the night. A terrible, despairing scream.

"Let it go, let it go," Doug said harshly. "We don't have time for it. Pompey, help me. she looks so white, Pomp."

"No," Margo said, belching water. "No, Doug. I just have to get some lake water out of myself. I'm all right."

"She's alive," Doug said, and she heard him sobbing, like a woman. A man crying?

"Don't touch me," she pleaded. "Don't touch me, for the Lord's sweet sake. I'm going to vomit …"

She screamed it.

"Stay away! Let me alone, stay away…let me get it out, once and forever…don't touch me!"

But he did. He lay down beside her, while she got a bellyfull out, and clamped his strong hands over her forehead when she said she was perishing of a headache, and after a while there was nothing but the two of them lying there, breathing hard, and Pompey standing over them, saying, "Mr. John, she be all right, won't she? Mr. John, don't let her die, please, Mr. John, don't let her die."

She looked up, her eyes crossed and unfocused, and said, "John?"

"Yes," he said calmly. "Come on now, you've got to get home. Just go limp, I'll lift you, don't fight it, that's the girl."

All the way home, in the car, the back seat, he held her. "Soon now," he kept saying. "Just a little way longer. Hold on, Margo."

"Yes."

"We're almost home."

"Okay, yes."

"How's your headache?"

"Pretty bad."

"We'll put you to bed, don't worry, some aspirin. You okay, dear?"

"Yes, I'm fine. Did you call me dear?"

"Why not, you're dear to me."

They got to the house. She could smell the house when they went in, the smell of age and must and beautiful memories. "But what about Norma?" she asked.

"We'll talk about that tomorrow."

"You're not kidding me," she said, quietly. "I heard her dying scream. She's dead, isn't she? All of them, dead. John, hold my hand, I'm so sad and lonely. Don't let me go. I don't want to be alone, I can't bear to be alone."

"I'm here," he said quietly. "Don't worry. I'll be here when you wake up, and long after that. Don't worry. I love you, Margo, I always have. Rest now. I love you. Pompey, get her clothes off. That's the girl."

Her eyes smarted and her stomach was working. "I think I have to throw up again," she said apologetically. "Pompey, can you get me to the bathroom?" And then the terrible scream came to her again.

"I heard Norma scream…where is she?"

"Hush," Pompey said, his dark face floating in front of her. "Hush now. I don't want to hear no more."

In the bathroom she got rid of some more lake water, and then Pompey helped her to bed. John stood there. He talked to Pompey, and Pompey said, "Now you just take these here pills, Miss Margo."

"What are they?" she asked, with only a kind of half vision.

"To make you sleep, that's all," John said, and the authority in his voice was exactly what she wanted.

She looked up trustingly. "I always knew she despised me, poor girl, but I don't want her to be dead. Can't you help her, can't you help?"

"It's too late for that," someone said, and the pin-wheels danced, and the circles widened, and then there was silence, complete and wonderful. "Oh, *now* I feel better," she heard herself say, and pillowed a head beneath a hand. The night closed around her; she was really so terribly tired.

"Are you there, John?" she asked.

He said, "Yes, I won't leave. Go to sleep now," and like a child she drifted off, because he was there, he had promised to stay there. "That's my girl," she heard someone say, and then that was all, but it was enough…it was enough …

CHAPTER FIFTEEN

Morning came, and with it the memory of what had happened. A bad taste in the mouth, a bile taste, and then a scream, echoing through the night. The water in her nose and mouth, the branch raised…Ben's voice …

All this, and then the mist cleared, and she looked up, saw him sitting there. "What are you doing in my room, Pompey?" she asked.

"I didn't want you to wake up to nothing," he said simply, and when her tears came, wiped them away with a tissue from her Kleenex box. They sat and held each other and then she asked him why he and John had come after her.

"Tell you the whole story," he said quietly. "Something happened the night you fell down them stairs. I plumb forgot the next morning, because I sleep hard, you know. Fact is, a little kitten mewed at the door, and I let her in. A cute little bugger, belongs a ways down to the Pipers', and since I feed her now and on occasion, she thinks she has two places to go for eats. She's a pretty little half Persian, and I took her into my bed. Then I heard something, so I got up, recalling them telephone calls you had, and wondering about all that. I went out to the big room, and everything seemed right enough.

"Then next morning you told me you fell down them stairs.

"It was then this old lame brain started putting two and two together. I had some ideas, not nice ideas, but I know Mr. John and I know Mr. Doug, and whatever their faults those are two good-hearted fellas, still young and raw, maybe, got a lot to learn, both of them. All right, the telephone calls. Mr. Douglas? Well, why? You were seeing each other, then why should he make nasty calls? Mr. John? If he wants to make a play for you, the way Mr.

Doug did, he could do that, couldn't he? Both of you in the same house?"

"Then who else?"

"There was, the way I saw it, only one other; Miss Norma. Since she was a child too, I know that girl. Smart in school, with all she had to live down, those parents nothing to brag about. But she had a brain and she used it. First it was Mr. Doug, but that didn't lead nowhere, so then it was Mr. John.

"The years, they come and go, and all them years she tries to pin down Mr. John. Not much opportunity in a small town like this, and she wanted more than some clerk in a store. Oh yes, she had ambitions. This house, she came here all the time, like it was her own, but Mr. John never paid her no mind. His mind too much on his work, for one thing.

"And then, last night, I was restless, kind of, because of those telephone calls you was getting. I couldn't sleep as good as usual. After a while I got up, wandered around a bit. It was when I came into the big room that I saw them lights again. Going away from the house, like that other night when you fell down the stairs, something funny about it. A car, late at night, going away, and at the time I thought about it. Who could be driving off so late at night? And then, last night, seeing the lights again, going off. I lit a lamp and saw the time. Little before ten. Mr. John went to the Tap Room of the John Adams house, say about nine thirty. And you? You went up to your room."

He spread his hands. "So what did I do? I went up to Mr. John's room, thinking he might of come back. I knocked at the door. No answer, so I went in.

"No Mr. John.

"So I go downstairs again, and look outside. His car gone from the driveway. But not only his car, your car too. That's funny, I think, and I race upstairs to your room. Knock at the door, no answer. I go in and no Miss Margo.

"At that point, only two things to do. Call Mr. John, maybe you go with him after all. I try the Tap Room. He comes to the phone. Says no, he's alone, you not with him.

"I don't like the sound of it, so next I call Mr. Doug. No answer. I try again, no answer. So I call Mr. John again. Lay it on the line. Tell him you're not home, not anywhere so far as I can see.

"Then he raised the ceiling. Screamed at me, he did. 'Can't you take better care of her?'

"I said he was right, I was a no-good old man. He was shouting at me, like God on a bad day. Hung up and a few minutes later he calls back.

" 'It's a long chance,' he says. 'But something come to me. When they was kids. She hit Margo on the head with a stick.'

" 'Who did that hittin',' I asked. 'Norma,' he said. 'She hit her and Margo almost drowned.'

"There was a buzzing on the phone and I started saying, 'Mr. John, you there?' and he said, in this funny voice, like he was choking, 'Let's try the lake.'

"I started to say something and he shouted at me again. 'You just get out there as fast as you can.' So I did. I got quick as a bunny into my old piece of tin and got out there."

He finished his story. "If not, Miss Margo, you been fished out of the water, dead as a doornail, with your eyes hanging open."

"Pompey," she said, whispering it. "I remember that day. I guess I didn't know much about jealousy then. Except I got the vibrations. I was the city girl, and they were paying a lot of attention to me, the twins. I didn't think much about it, I liked it, obviously. But she must have suffered…watching them fight over me."

"She was bad, a bad girl."

"No, not really, Pomp. She was a victim. I'm sure she loved John, and she wanted something from life. I don't blame her, I never will."

"I do," he said implacably. "I saw that face of Miss Vicky, purple, her tongue hanging out. Who's to ever know now if she died natural?"

She stared at him.

"What *do* you mean?" she asked breathlessly.

"Could have put a pillow over her poor head," he said.

"*Norma?*"

"Day in, day out. Year in, year out. Came a time, maybe, when that girl went plumb crazy. Thought, I'll end it, I can't stand this no more. I just remember her face, Miss Margo. Like a fish pulled out of water. The eyes gogging out. It could have been that way."

John saying, "Tell her, Norma." She had gulled him, pretending weakness where there was none.

Mr. Bach: "She never had a bad day."

And Norma, sad-eyed: "John, she's failing ..."

A still strong woman, looking into the face of hate, seeing the inexorable advance of the hands coming toward her ...

She had a good life, Margo thought, *Please let me remember that...she had a good life. Christ, let me always remember that ...*

"Don't cry like that," Pompey said, distressed, holding her. "Please, Miss Margo, don't cry like that."

And then the hands had choked out her life. And she had seen that it would happen, hence the palindrome. "Don't," Pompey said, pleading. "You'll make yourself sick, Miss Margo."

• • •

Her body was fished out of the water that afternoon. Bloated, eyes open and befogged, hair tangled with water-weed and slime. That beautiful face. The hooks dragged her up, laid her on the ground, a pitiful thing, dead and swollen from the water that had devoured her. "Got tangled in some hell-vines," the townspeople were told. "Good swimmer too, but these things happen."

The casket was closed. She was unrecognizable; it was better that way. Who wanted to see such a sight?

And so the casket was closed, not to offend. There were a great many carnations: they had been Norma's favorite flower.

· · ·

There were visitors all through the day. Old Mrs. Pride, the Minister, and several ladies from the Women's League of the Methodist Church, bringing pastry and jellies and fudge brownies. The small son of a neighbor brought a whole Virginia ham, with cloves. "She'd of come," he explained about his mother, through the braces on his teeth. " 'Cept she's almost to term, there's another child on the way."

He was darling, with soft brown eyes and a peachy skin, accepting with downcast eyes but a dimpled cheek, Margo's kiss and Pompey's pat on the bottom.

Abner Zeiss called, saying what a horrible thing, and quoting poetry. "Over a monstrous sea without a bourn ..."

And Norma Calvet was buried the next day.

There were no more telephone calls from that day on.

Douglas called, his arms filled with fruits and vegetables and grapes and half a side of beef. "I was always fond of Norma," he said quietly. "We all thought she was doing so well. I don't know whether anyone told you, but she spent a year in Forrest Hill, had electric shock, but seemed to recover very well, and made a life for herself."

So you see, you find out little by little, Margo thought when he went off. Beautiful Norma, with her problems and heartaches, had at some time in her life spent a year in a mental institution. *And it was I who triggered the reaction,* Margo thought, *I who was the cause of her regression.*

Could she ever forget that?

At six o'clock, John came home. Margo was curled up on the camel-backed sofa, wan and tired. She said, "Hello, John," and he said,

"Hello, Margo," and gave her a quick look. "You've been wondering about Ben, I imagine. He's in the hospital, I gave him a rather rough going-over, but he's alive and well. Only he'll never set foot on this place again."

He stood there, at the liquor cart, a hand dashing back his dark hair, and then poured the drinks he made. They sat almost silent, and the cooking smells drifted in from the kitchen. But after a while she had to speak, and said, "John, I just want to say that I'm not going to use this house. It's yours, you deserve it. You stuck, through thick and thin, through the years. So the house is yours, John, because when I turn it over to the Historical Society I'll insist you be curator. As a matter of fact it will be a *sine qua non.*" She looked up. "John, I owe you my life. But I don't belong here. All those years were…years ago. I'm so…so wracked about Norma, and you must have loved her. In spite of what Pompey said. I'm sure you loved Norma, and I do understand."

He got up and stared down at her. "Why, you don't understand one single thing!" he said harshly. "Are you blind, then? I *never* loved Norma! I pitied her, wanted the best for her…but I never loved her, nor did I give her any proof that I did. She tried with Doug and she tried with me. But for God's sake that poor darling was pitiable, *pitiable!* It was always you, for both of us, Douglas and myself. You were the wonderful unattainable. I know you've fallen for my brother, and it's bad luck for me. He has the charisma, the bravado. Me? I was always the boy who stayed close to home, taking care of her, Aunt Vicky. I know I'm no prize. I can't help what I am. But just don't say…that…that …"

He got up and went to the liquor cart. "You'll be ready for another drink," he said thickly.

She didn't answer, simply sat looking at him as he pushed his thick, dark hair back with an impatient hand, and didn't fail to notice that as he filled her glass he spilled some liquid, and that the fingers that wiped up the spill were trembling. *They're both beautiful young men*, she thought, and God forgive her if she ever put down John as a clod. Why, he had lived here, through boyhood and manhood, keeping the home fires burning, and as she looked at him from across the room he seemed to grow in stature in her eyes. No European vacations? Why? Because Aunt Vicky had been too old to travel. He had kept the going concern, with good will and good nature.

Charisma? Anyone could have charisma. But character? How many persons had character?

"Here you are," he said, coming back and handing her the glass.

She said, "Thanks, John," and looked at him, kept looking at him, until he grew uneasy and said, "We might have some music."

He got up and turned on the radio. The strains of *"Wien, Wien, nur du allein"* filled the room. He sat down again, quietly—John did everything quietly—and crossed his long, lithe legs.

There was a long, protracted silence. Then she said, "Aren't you ever going to get married, John?"

"Possibly not."

"Why?"

"Because there was always only one person."

"What's that person's name?"

"Oh, Margo," he said angrily. "I just told you. It was always you, and now will you please drink up and for sake let me be?"

"You don't mean to say you're still in love with me?"

"Yes, but don't give it a thought. Undoubtedly I'll be the best man, keeping a "stiff upper lip. Please don't say anything more."

"Well, of course I'll say something more," she said, putting down her glass. "If you don't kiss me, I won't ever know what I missed."

He pushed back his hair again, looking angry, even threatening. Then he too put down his glass. "You're making fun of me," he said.

"No, certainly not. If you don't let me know how you feel, I can't possibly imagine what it would be like. And if I can't imagine what it would be like, we're out of luck, you and I."

It happened rather quickly. Then he was there, beside her. Then he was holding her. Then kissing her. Mouth to mouth, body against body. "Why, John," she tried to say, but couldn't tear herself away from him. It was just that dazzling time before the sun set, so that gold shot in through the Deerfield blinds, and she had to close her eyes against the blinding beauty of it, and she knew that she had found her home at last, here, in this beloved old house.

Pompey, poking his head in, said hastily, "Oh, excuse me, you two, just that dinner's almost ready."

"Dinner's almost ready," she said dreamily, and wound her arms around John, now knowing that she would end her days here, with this man she had known as a boy and who had fished her out of the lake water and given her back life. They would have children, and their children would have children, and the House on the Hill would endure into other centuries, other times, while they grew old and gray and died their natural deaths.

But before that —

Before that would be the begetting of them, in one of the tester beds, love children, love children. "John," she said, when he got up hastily. "Why are you leaving me?"

"Because discretion is the greater part of valor," he told her, flushed, and stirred the pitcher of martinis.

Then Pompey poked his head in the room again. "Scuse it," he apologized. "Just that the pot roast's getting overcooked. Sorry to intrude." He added, somewhat questioning, "The rest can wait, can't it?"

"The rest can wait, can't it?" John asked, with a quick look at Margo, who said yes, indeed, the rest could wait…for a while …

For a while.

At Christmas, they would trim a tree together, and exchange presents, two people in love, and see out the seasons in this fine old house. And, as it had all those years ago, her aunt's voice seemed to speak to her, warm and friendly and enthusiastic. "Well, then, here you are, Margo, everything set for you, just what I would have wanted. You must grow up, you know, you're no longer a child, and if you want to be a good wife you must find wisdom. You will have patience, that's the secret of it all, Margo, my dearly beloved…patience…patience."

CHAPTER SIXTEEN

"You are not to think about it," John says, getting out of bed as he sees her standing at the window, restless in the night "I forbid you to think about it."

But she will. In time even that terrible memory will fade. Not entirely, for it will always be there, in her mind, the exquisite face unrecognizable, the dewy eyes popping, the hair like seaweed, the arms and legs swollen stumps: *It could have been me*, Margo thinks.

"Darling, come back to bed."

She goes back to bed, holding him, for in the morning there will be a tour, and they will eat a hasty breakfast, after which she will follow him, listening. "In the year 1659, a band of English pioneers, following the lordly Hudson upstream in search of fertile lands, paused when they reached a place where the river seems to linger to embrace the Sterling intervale, before it breaks through Mount Tom and Michford and flows to the sea ..."

The tourists, from every part of New York State, follow him, murmuring, touching with light and reverent fingers, the artifacts of another age. The House on the Hill, beautiful and timeless, stands on its summit, the sun flaming through its windows, making them golden and glorious, and the mansard roof, innocent of any television antenna, is outlined against the blue upstate sky, and the lilac bushes, fragrant and purple, blossom beside the Georgian doorway. And a man named John Michaels shows visitors through the house.

They go off, in buses, and John reaches for his wife's hand. "Well, how did I do today?" he asks.

"Very good. Have I told you, lately, that I'm madly in love with you?"

"Are you, darling?"

They don't need to talk it over. They go upstairs, to the master bedroom, to hold each other. Pompey calls up after an hour. "Dinner soon," his voice says. "Last call for dinner."

And the trees shiver in the breeze, the bushes quiver with life, the House on the Hill stands fast, a bridge between past and present.

Yes, and there was a whole life ahead.

And because she was New England bred, she remembers the lines. She gets up, after kissing her young husband, and remembers the lines. There is a smell of asparagus and pork, and she remembers the lines. John gets up too, and they rock together, so in love, so in love. And she remembers the lines. They say, out of habit now, "Darling, darling."

And she remembers the lines.

A woman died, and left, part and parcel, a house with memories, a house whose beginnings started two centuries ago. She thinks of that, and remembers the lines. They are now part of her very being.

> *"The woods are lovely, dark and deep*
> *But I have promises to keep,*
> *And miles to go before I sleep,*
> *And miles to go before I sleep…"*

A Sneak Peek from Crimson Romance
(From *In Plain Sight* by Susanne Matthews)

Misty Starr stared at herself in the full-length mirror in the small dressing room she shared with the other women in the cast and started to laugh, her voice as crisp and clear as a crystal bell. She shook her head from side to side in resignation.

"Martha has got to be kidding, right? I look like a beach cabana," she said, referring the deep pink and white, vertically striped robe she wore that hung far too loosely on her small frame. "I know Micah said I had to stand out, but is this really the look he was going for? I thought stripes were supposed to make you look taller."

The costume consisted of a white under-tunic, covered by a long, striped robe, topped with a deep pink shawl that was meant to cover her head as well. Instead of being light and airy, the fabric used for the shawl was thick and stiff and did not sit well on the long, dark brown wig that covered her short hair. The wig itself was loose and had a tendency to slip, since Martha seemed unable to secure it tightly to her head. With the shawl pinned to the wig, the whole thing had a tendency to slide backward, and holding her head up so the whole mess didn't slip off was a chore.

"Come on; it's not that bad," said Amber, one of the friends Misty had made since moving to Pine Falls who was currently trying valiantly not to laugh at her. "You look cute! I look like I'm wearing a beach towel, and a really ugly one at that." The tight, narrow stripes in alternating shades of green, brown, mustard, and tan were not the nicest combination of colors, and the robe had a distinctly dowdy look to it.

"No one is going to take me seriously in this outfit," said Misty. "Does she honestly think Mary Magdalene went around wearing pink stripes, looking like a hospital candy striper or an escapee from a clown convention? The only things missing are the big red shoes, the fright wig, and the rubber nose! They probably didn't even have pink yarn for weaving back then. Why couldn't she just let me wear navy or brown instead? At least your costume looks more like what I would have expected a disciple to wear—mine, not so much." She turned away from the mirror just as a knock at the door announced company.

"Are you decent?"

"Yes!" shouted Amber. "We're almost ready if you've come to chase us up the stairs."

The door opened to reveal three people—Micah Jones, the director of the Pine Hill Community Theater Group, his wife, Laura, and an unknown man. With Micah in the lead, they entered the room.

Misty smiled at her friends and stared at what was by far the most striking man she'd ever seen. She felt the heat of desire curl in her stomach, a sensation she'd been certain she'd never feel again. *This is a hell of a time to be dressed like this,* she thought. *The first man I've seen in five years that I find attractive and look at me. What I wore here was nothing special but at least it fit me properly.*

Laura rushed to get into costume, while the men stood beside the door. Misty could see the male cast gathered outside in the hall. Whoever the unfamiliar man was, he was important to Micah, and that meant he was necessary for the production of the play. Maybe he was the unknown financial backer Micah had mentioned, the one who was covering the costs of the production so that all the money raised by the community could go to the local clinic.

The stranger was tall, well over six feet, with short, dark hair that curled at the neckline, attesting to the fact that it needed a trim. There was a recently healed, jagged scar along the right side of his forehead that ran from the top of his hairline to his eyebrow, but instead of marring his beauty, the mark made him seem more intriguing and reminded her of a similar scar on a young wizard from a series of books she'd loved in her teens. He was clean-shaven, with a Roman nose, and had a generous mouth with full lips currently turned down in a frown.

He wore black, brushed-denim jeans, which molded to his muscular legs like a second skin, a charcoal gray shirt, and a black, kid-leather jacket. His feet were shod in black leather loafers. Everything about him, from the way he held his head to his shoes, screamed, "Look at me! I'm somebody!" Misty shivered. Whoever he was, he didn't seem at all pleased to be here.

Based on his austere clothing and the scowl on his face, Misty decided he must be a serious-minded individual, and from his glare, she'd bet he was no more impressed with her costume than she was. Then again, it might have been her tactless comment that had soured his disposition. For all she knew, if he was the money behind this particular staging of *Jesus Christ Superstar*, she might have struck a nerve. He might even have chosen the color and the fabric with economy in mind. She knew Martha had bought up all the remnants she could find in town.

It was her turn to frown. Fabulous guys like this were either gay or married. Hell, Martha, the wardrobe director, might even be his wife. Hadn't Amber said Martha's husband was a trust-fund hottie? Well, this man was most definitely hot, and the clothes he wore so well shrieked money. The unexpected shot to her libido momentarily had her forgetting who and what she was. Reality quickly reasserted itself.

Misty had been living in Pine Falls for eight months now, and she really didn't want to move again. She and her daughter, Debbie, were happy here. This man was a stranger, and strangers spelled danger. For more than four years, she'd run from relationships and people, including confident, powerful men like this one, avoiding friendships and commitment. She'd kept to herself, believing that if she did, she'd be safe. It hadn't worked, and good people had died. What made her think stepping outside the box to become a member of this community and make friends here would be a wise thing to do? At the moment, it looked as if she might have made a colossal error.

Her mind focused on the present and the gorgeous stranger who reminded her of a sleek black cat, whose stormy, gray-blue eyes seemed to look right through her. She shuddered. This man was dangerous. He walked with the grace and ease of a panther on the prowl, wary of everything and everyone in the room. He might look like he could purr under the right circumstances, but at the moment, it was more likely he'd rip your throat out if he got the chance.

Micah walked over to the center of the room with the stranger following close behind him. She wanted to look away, but she couldn't seem to get her eyes to cooperate with her brain. She was like a moth drawn to the flame, unable to escape its destiny.

"Ladies and gentlemen," Micah said as he and the newcomer approached the center of the room, capturing the attention of the female cast and the men who'd filed into the dressing room. "I have some good news and some bad news for you tonight." The cast gave a group groan. It seemed as if this musical was cursed; they'd been practicing since September, and every time they thought they had some glitch worked out, something else went wrong. In fact, it had been one of those minor disasters that had resulted in Misty's joining the company.

In September, Amos, the agent who'd brought them to Pine Falls, had helped her purchase a small, two-story house just down the street from his. With his help, she'd established a solid cover story, and she and her daughter had fallen in love with their new home, the first real one they'd had since she'd made the fateful decision to testify against the Irish mob. Amos had put in a good word and helped her get a job as secretary at the local elementary school.

She'd been talked into joining the theater group after Amber had heard her sing karaoke the night of the school's Christmas party. Her rendition of "I Love Rock and Roll" had brought the room to its feet. Since the theater group's best soprano had been transferred to Oregon, they hadn't been able to find a replacement. Misty's voice was just what they needed to fill the void.

Although Misty had wanted the role, she'd declined because she hadn't felt right asking Beryl, Amos's wife, to babysit. When she'd mentioned it to Charlotte, her widowed neighbor who had a four-year-old of her own, she'd offered to babysit for Misty.

After more than four years of running, hiding, working, and looking after Debbie, Misty had needed some "me" time and had finally agreed. She enjoyed being part of the theater group and had even been persuaded to go on a couple of dates, but no one had pushed her buttons.

She shook her head and tried to focus on what Micah was saying because the man beside him worried her. Who was he? What did he want? Why was he here? The fear she'd cultivated all these years ate at her.

"I got a call from Jolene on Monday. Everything is fine, but she fell down a few steps at the mall last weekend. She claimed she was pushed—we all know how Jolene likes to exaggerate—and her doctor has orders bed rest until after the baby is born, which means I needed to find someone who could handle the music quickly since we open next week. By the way, Jolene needs peace and quiet, so don't all go rushing over to see her tomorrow, okay?"

"What are you, a mind reader?" asked Amber.

"No," he replied, "Laura told me to say that. As a doctor, she knows what Jolene needs better than I do. Anyway, I'd like you all to meet Nick Anthony. He's a retired musician and has experience with this type of performance. He'll be taking over. The rest of you can move upstairs to the stage and get ready, but I'd ask Misty and Amber to wait a second." The men turned and left the room.

Micah took Nick by the arm and all but dragged him across the floor to where they stood a little apart from the rest of the cast.

"Nick, I'd like you to meet Misty Starr and Amber Collins, two of my Marys. Amber has the role of Mary, the mother of Jesus, and Misty is Mary Magdalene; she's the one I mentioned earlier."

Misty pulled together every shred of self-control she possessed and stuck out her hand to shake his. She could do this; she could touch this man and remain unscathed. He was a stranger; she would survive—she had to.

"Good to meet you ladies," Nick said, completely ignoring the extended hand. "I'll speak with each of you later, if not tonight then before the next rehearsal. This run-through will give me an opportunity to hear your voices, and then I'll see if I have any pointers for you. I'll be recording some of the rehearsal to help me with that." With a curt nod, he followed Micah to the door and waited while Micah talked to one of the stagehands.

Upset by his lack of common courtesy, Misty withdrew her hand. Although he frightened her, he also intrigued her. His voice, with a slight accent she knew couldn't be Irish—she'd recognize an Irish accent anywhere—was smooth, like warm caramel, and didn't fit the aloof look he gave her and the frown marring his face. She shivered. What had she ever done to make him look at her that way? And why is he staring at her?

Could he be one of them? Could he be a trained assassin hoping to earn what she knew was a fat bounty on her head? She had no doubt he could be a dangerous man if crossed. She'd learned to look for the underlying signs of violence in everyone she met. She saw repressed anger and frustration in Mr. Anthony, *if* that was his real name. Not recognizing those signs five years ago had almost cost her her life. At first glance she'd thought him a stranger, but slowly she realized there was something familiar about him, and when she gave credence to that, it agitated the acidic butterflies that had invaded her stomach.

"Well, that was rude and awkward," huffed Amber, keeping her voice just above a whisper. "He completely ignored your offer to shake his hand! Maybe he's one of those germaphobes—you know, doesn't shake hands, afraid he might catch something. You know the type. Or he could be some kind of superstar who refuses to let common people touch him. Either way, he's a jerk!" She snorted and stared at Nick as if he were a parasite.

"Don't let it bother you, Amber." Misty fought to keep her terror in check. "I'm not offended. I've known more than my fair share of rude people, and although he may not have shaken my hand, he did speak to us. I just wish he'd stop staring at me like that."

Despite everything, he attracted her physically as no man had ever done, and she longed to reach out and touch him, but the way he stared at her—the look on his face—made her blood run cold. He stood by the door waiting for Micah, a scowl firmly fixed on his face. Frustrated, on the verge of panic, she fought the childish urge to stick out her tongue at him or flip him the bird, anything to provoke a response from him. Why was he focused on her like this?

Laura, Micah's wife as well as Pine Hills's only doctor and a member of the play's chorus, had finished putting on her costume and came over to join them. "Well, you've met the new music director. What do you think? I can't imagine how Micah convinced him to do this; I've been after Nick for more than a year to get out and do something," she said matter-of-factly. "This is the last thing I thought he'd ever do. Well?"

Misty felt the butterflies settle, and she relaxed. He wasn't a stranger; he'd been in Pine Falls longer than she had. She'd let that wild imagination of hers conjure up all kinds of demons. If Debbie had inherited her imagination, it's no wonder she has nightmares. She looked at the man who'd captured her interest. Now that she wasn't seeing him as a potential threat, she noticed the stiffness of his shoulders, the way his hands fisted at his sides, and the way he held himself, tense and alert. She saw that the grimace he wore wasn't one of anger, but of worry. She recognized the emotion; it was one with which she was intimately familiar— that fear of failure, of not being good enough, of being rejected.

Feeling more like herself, she smiled, prepared to offer him an olive branch, but although he was looking straight at her, he ignored her. She shrugged.

Too bad, she thought. *I think we could have been friends.*

She'd realized since she'd arrived in Pine Falls that friends were important—far more necessary than she'd ever thought they could be. Without them, a person was lonely and lost, the way she'd been until recently. Now, she'd fight for the life she had built here.

"I think he's rude," Amber answered Laura, interrupting Misty's musing, this time speaking loud enough to be overheard, and Nick turned toward her. "Look at him staring at Misty as if she were a cockroach. I've a good mind to go over there and say something."

"Shush, he'll hear you, Amber," warned Misty.

A deaf man could hear you, she thought, embarrassed that her friend should take the snub so personally.

"Well, it's true." Amber snorted. "You're too nice. One of these days someone is going to stomp on your parade, mark my word. You need to learn to stand up for yourself."

Misty was chilled by Amber's premonition. Hadn't she been stomped on enough already?

"Amber!" Laura's voice was filled with reprimand. "He isn't staring at Misty or at anyone else. Didn't Micah say anything? I guess not. What is it about men and stating the obvious? Nick is blind."

Misty watched color suffuse Amber's cheeks as her own grew hot. She felt awful. She looked straight at Nick's mesmerizing gray-blue eyes and noticed they were unfocused, the way eyes tended to be when someone was daydreaming. Why hadn't she seen that earlier? Being so worried about her safety had made her oblivious to the fact that not only was he *not* staring at her, he probably hadn't even realized she was there.

"Hell, Laura, I feel like such an ass," hissed Amber. "Why isn't he wearing dark glasses? For Pete's sake, the man should have the decency to give us a few clues. It isn't as if we're all clairvoyant."

Micah asked the remaining cast members to go up to the stage, and as they moved from the dressing room to the theater, Misty berated herself. Hadn't she learned the hard way not to judge a book by its cover? Hadn't the mistake she'd made trusting Kevin O'Hara been enough to convince her not to let her eyes deceive her? She felt the need to say something to Nick, to apologize to him for Amber's rude comments, but before she could approach him, Micah called the cast to order and explained how the night's rehearsal would proceed.

"Places, everyone," called Micah. "Nick, whenever you're ready."

Misty watched as Nick removed his jacket and set it on the floor beside him. He placed something in his pocket, walked over to the eighty-eight key digital piano and sat down on the bench. He spread out his arms and spanned the keys with his fingers. Mesmerized by his actions, she watched as his hands, with beautifully long tapered fingers—what her mother would have called the hands of an artist—brushed over the keys.

"Here," Nick said, removing what he'd put in his pocket earlier and handing it to Micah, who placed a small, personal recording device near the speaker. Tonight they would only use the hanging microphones, but on performance nights, the soloists would all wear individual mikes.

"Nick assures me this will pick up all your voices nicely; no need to sing or speak louder than you normally would. I can assure you, when it comes to music, this guy knows all the tricks and loves his toys."

The cast laughed softly, but Misty could tell many of them were as worried as she was that they might not live up to a retired musician's standards since none of them was anything other than an amateur—well, maybe she had more experience, but that was a secret she couldn't share with anyone. Would he realize she'd had more than a little voice training? Micah had said he was a retired musician, but he hadn't stated what kind of musician. Misty watched as he familiarized himself with the instrument he'd play.

He must play by ear, she thought. She'd known a lot of musicians over the years who played by ear, but not all of them could pull off something of this magnitude without a musical score. As a pianist, no doubt he'd be fine, but the musical had a forty-piece high school orchestra backing up the vocalists, not the seasoned performers you'd find in a professional presentation of the musical. It wouldn't be easy to conduct the band if he couldn't follow the score.

Why Micah wanted him to fill in for Jolene she couldn't imagine, but since the high school music teacher was unable to continue, perhaps there hadn't been anyone else available on short notice. Substitute teachers could fill in at the high school, but this took someone with extensive knowledge of music. Since many of the tickets for the performances had been presold, and the presentation was a much-needed fundraiser for the local medical clinic, they had to go ahead as planned.

She sighed and allowed her usual fatalism to take over. This was just another glitch. There wasn't anything they could do about it. She'd play her part, sing her songs, and hope it all worked. That twinge of fear she'd had that someone might recognize her in the play gnawed at her for a few seconds, but then who from her past would come to Pine Falls, New York, to watch amateur theater? Although the small town was in a tourist area, it didn't attract the crowds the way Lake Placid, Saranac Lake, and Tupper Lake did. Potsdam and Canton, the two largest urban areas nearby, were both college towns, but it was unlikely anyone from New York City would see her in sleepy little Pine Falls. Amos was probably right; it wasn't anything to worry about.

www.ingramcontent.com/pod-product-compliance
Lightning Source LLC
Chambersburg PA
CBHW010303100726
47904CB00011B/2721